C000230680

ONE
OF US
IS LYING

SALLY
CLINE

GOLDEN
BOOKS

ONE
OF US
IS LYING

SALLY
CLINE

**SHORT FICTION and
RADIO DRAMA**

GOLDEN BOOKS

This collection first published in Great Britain in
2013 by
GOLDEN BOOKS
www.goldenbooks.co.uk

Golden Books
47 Searle Street
Cambridge CB4 3DB

A CIP Catalogue of this book is available from the
British Library .

Paperback ISBN: 978-0-9573079-3-3
Kindle ebook ISBN: 978-0-9573079-4-0
epub ebook ISBN: 978-0-9573079-5-7

Cover photo: ©istockphoto/Panupong Roopyai

Cover design and typeset by
www.chandlerbookdesign.co.uk

Printed in Great Britain by
PrintonDemand-Worldwide.

CONTENTS

STORIES

RADIO DRAMA

NOTE ON AUTHOR

Sally Cline, Fellow of The Royal Society of Arts and Advisory Fellow of the Royal Literary Fund, is the author of 11 books including biographies of Radclyffe Hall (shortlisted for a LAMBDA award), the award-winning Zelda Fitzgerald, and forthcoming January 2014 *Dashiell Hammett: Man of Mystery* (Arcade Books USA). She has now completed a biographical study of Lillian Hellman.

She is one of the UK Judges for the 2013 H.W. Fisher Best First Biography Prize and is co-series editor of Bloomsbury's 9 volume series of books on writing, for which she has co-authored two volumes; one on life writing and one on literary non-fiction.

Chapter 5 of her first novel *The Visitor* is on the web in issue 11 of *The International Literary Quarterly* for which she is a Consulting Editor. Her short fiction for print and radio has won prizes from the BBC and Raconteur and been shortlisted for the Asham Award. She has received a Hawthornden Fellowship, and won the Hosking Houses Trust Fellowship for Women Writers over 40.

She lives in Cambridge, has taught at Cambridge University, was Writer in Residence at Anglia Ruskin

University, has judged and mentored for the Arts Council Escalator programme and currently for the prestigious Gold Dust mentoring scheme. She has degrees and Masters from Durham and Lancaster Universities and an Honorary Doctorate in writing internationally.

SALLY CLINE'S PREVIOUS BOOKS

BIOGRAPHIES and BOOKS ABOUT LIFE WRITING

Life Writing: Biography Autobiography and Memoir: A Writers' and Artists' Companion (with Carole Angier)

Dashiell Hammett: Man of Mystery

Zelda Fitzgerald: The Tragic, Meticulously Researched Biography of the Jazz Age's High Priestess

Zelda Fitzgerald: Her Voice in Paradise

Radclyffe Hall: A Woman called John

LITERARY NON-FICTION BOOKS

Writing Literary Non-Fiction: A Writers' and Artists' Companion (with Midge Gillies)

Couples: Scene from the Inside

Lifting the Taboo: Women, Death and Dying

Women, Celibacy and Passion

Just Desserts: Women and Food

Reflecting Men at Twice their Natural Size (with Dale Spender)

EDITED BOOKS

As Series Editor:

Crime and Thriller Writing: A Writers' and Artists' Companion
(Michelle Spring and Laurie King)

Writing Children's Fiction: A Writers' and Artists' Companion
(Yvonne Coppard and Linda Newbery)

Writing Historical Fiction: A Writers' and Artists' Companion
(Celia Brayfield and Duncan Sprott. Forthcoming Dec 2013)

As Editor:

Memoirs of Emma Courtney (Mary Hays)

BOOKS and JOURNALS WHERE STORIES PREVIOUSLY PUBLISHED

Thanks to the following publications where some stories
from this collection have already appeared:

"The Passenger" appeared in *Fen and Ink*: *Anthology of
New Writing from East Cambridgeshire,* ed. Edward Storey,
1995. It was winner of the BBC Radio Cambridgeshire/
BBC East/Eastern Arts Board short story contest,
February 1993. Winner of BBC short story contest 1994.

"A Small Number" appeared in *Mordecai's First Brush
With Love.* New Stories by Jewish Women in Britain, eds.
Phillips and Baraitser. Loki Books, London 1997. It was
revised and performed at Hawthornden Castle during the
author's Hawthornden Fellowship 2003.

"The Green Bin" appeared in *The Pottersfield Portfolio,* vol 10. New Writing from Atlantic Canada, 1988.

"Daisy Writing Letters" published as "Letters", *New Fiction,* vol 12, issue 3. New Fiction Publications, Spring 1994. Published as "Letters" in *Second Shift* Arts Magazine, UK, Summer 1994.

"Return Match" appeared in *The Pottersfield Portfolio,* vol 12. New Writing from Atlantic Canada, September 1991.

"The Very Thought of You" was published as "Isolated Incident" in *The West in Her Eye,* ed. Rachel Lever. Pyramid Press, UK, 1995

"Recent Changes at a Canadian University" published as "Changes" under pseudonym Daisy Kempe in *Naming the Waves,* ed. Christian McEwen. Virago, 1988.

"Remembrance Sunday" appeared in *More Serious Pleasure. Lesbian Erotic Stories and Poetry,* ed. Sheba Collective, Sheba Feminist Press. Published under pseudonym Daisy Kempe, 1990.

"The Removal" appeared in *Second Shift* Arts Magazine, UK, Summer 1994. It appeared in *Fingerprints. An Anthology of Crime Shorts,* ed. Suzi Blair. New Fiction publications, UK, 1992. It appeared in *The Other Newspaper,* Nova Scotia, Canada, 1991.

"Paintboxed In" appeared in *The Pottersfield Portfolio,* vol 12. New Writing from Atlantic Canada, September 1991. Also published in *The Other Newspaper,* Nova Scotia, Canada, 1991. Also published in *Second Shift* Arts Magazine, UK, 1994.

"October Photograph" published in *New Fiction,*
New Fiction Publications, UK, Spring 1994.

"Café Memorial" published in *Raconteur Anthology.*
Prize winning story. Raconteur Publications, UK,
September 1994.

The Passenger in Pink. Radio play. LAB/LBC London
Radio Playwrights' Festival 1993 . Shortlisted June 1994.

This book is dedicated to

BA SHEPPARD

and

(RUBY) JILL DAWSON

ACKNOWLEDGEMENTS

My major acknowledgement is to the team at Golden Books for their generous editorial eye and excellence especially Chris Carling and Glenn Jobson.

The typing and collating of the material was done with efficiency and grace by Angie North and Holly Jobson.

A volume of thanks goes to Tracy Baker who offered me Atlantic Lodge in exquisite Sennen Cornwall to finish the manuscript in peace silence and beauty.

Mighty appreciation to Anne Helmreich for her constant transatlantic calls, help and encouragement.

Great gratitude for years of enthusiasm and strength goes to Marmoset Adler (almost daily support), Vic Smith (unending lively optimism), Rosemary Smith (careful considered wise advice) and to Kathy Bowles, Jane Shackman, Sally Lawrence, Frankie (Frances) Borzello, Neil McKenna, Michelle Spring, Carole Angier, Colette Paul, Alan French, Rachel Calder, Katharine McMahon, Anne Gurnett, Midge Gillies, Richard Baker, Eleanor Vale, Marion Stewart and the wonderful Harris team: Jonathan, Joan, Noam and Danya.

(Ruby) Jill Dawson has inspired me for years and I cannot thank her sufficiently for her affectionate advice over turning these stories finally into a book.

Again precious thanks to Ba Sheppard who has been there for me and the writing every inch of the way over 35 years.

PREFACE

I wrote these largely linked stories over two decades. The links were not purposeful. Only when I decided to gather up most of those that had already been published in magazines and anthologies and place them into a single volume did I realise that many of them were in some way linked by protagonists or settings or the dark emotions beneath the polished surfaces and glittering conversations. A secondary character in one story appears as a central character in another. The few stand-alone fictions have different protagonists but, as I wrote them, the same symbols edged those stories towards others already linked.

They are all concerned with love, loss, longing and betrayal. They twist around feelings of unease. I hope that the small disturbances of contemporary or even suburban life will invoke in the reader echoes of historic violence or ancient fears.

Though some backdrops return readers to the era and climate of Nazi Germany most actions and settings take place in areas I know well such as London, Cambridge, Brighton, Cornwall, Scotland, Oxford in England as well as Canada, Texas and several Greek Islands.

STORIES

THE PASSENGER

Near the end of the train a woman sat alone, looking anxiously out of the window. The fingers of her right hand unsteadily clenched and unclenched a paper cup of coffee on the table in front of her. The fingers of the other hand scratched nervously at the print of a half-folded newspaper. Was she trying to tear the words away from their page? Her lips moved rhythmically as if in time to the scratching. Occasionally she turned her head as if responding to another passenger, but there was no-one else inside the compartment.

You are giving yourself away I thought. String bags and plastic carriers will not contain you. You are giving yourself away. Cheap at the price. I am someone who has always avoided bargains.

Self preservation warned me to hurry on. The woman was what the grey days of winter had hinted as a summer possibility. I am someone who enjoys the snow. Nip in the air. Tingle of frost. I must work to prevent it.

At that moment a shaft of late afternoon sun came out and caught on the red lights of her greying hair, and then shifted to the extraordinary blaze of her dress. It was liquorice-all-sorts pink, shot silk, falling in folds abundantly over the drab grey green seat.

"Dreadful clash with that hair," I muttered. "She probably used henna. Did it herself. Badly at that. Certainly not a dress in which to travel on the four o'clock to Whittlesford. The woman has no style at all."

Faces on a train are easily forgotten. Why can I not take my eyes away from you? Your cheeks are grey, like the smoke smudged window I stare through.

As if fixed by the shaft of sunlight, focused first on her bent red streaked hair, then on the shaking fingers alternately tearing at the newspaper, clenching at the cup, I stood immovable watching the woman through a dirty pane. She looked up and caught my inquisitive patronising gaze. My idle penetration. Her piercing blue eyes with an ancient tired resignation accepted the hostile mixture of curiosity and indifference in mine. She bent her head again.

My ignorance of you stands outside my knowledge of you. Circle upon circle. Binding me. I do not want that.

I hastened further down the platform. I needed the solitude of an empty carriage. Needed the peace of the sixty minute journey back to the country. Hurriedly I walked on. Then back. Up and down the platform. Up and down. Casting anxious eyes on the clock. Speculating between this carriage and that.

Already I knew I should go back. I who had yearned for an empty compartment to myself was now desperate that the one with the woman in lurid pink silk should quickly fill up. I moved nearer. I was able to monitor the spaces. Several middle-aged men got in briskly, then a girl in a spotted headscarf, a tired mother with two fractious toddlers, and a young woman with purple punky hair. I was safe. I should be able to slip unnoticed into whatever was the remaining seat.

The woman, tired but strangely compelling in the liquorice pink silk looked up as I entered the carriage. She took a folded newspaper off the seat opposite her.

"I saved it," she muttered, apparently to no-one in particular but the searching blue eyes closed in steadily on me. "Horrid having to stand all the way, isn't it." Nobody answered her.

The men rustled Times and Independents. The punk was roping black beads around her skinny arms. The mother was quietening the elder child with nougat, while saying feverishly: "Nougat is very bad for your teeth, Jonny, you really shouldn't". Gently she rocked the younger child, a small girl with freckles and a large brace on her teeth. Was she weaned on nougat I wondered, as uneasily I slid into the seat the passenger had left empty for me.

The woman with hair more grey than red was drinking now from the shaking plastic cup. The train had not yet moved off. There was a stillness in the compartment as we all waited for the familiar noise of the guard slamming shut the doors before the train began its comfortable jolting pace. The stillness was broken by the woman's uneven jerky breathing.

My eyes, unwillingly fastened on to hers, pulled away from thoughts as plastic and shaky as her cup. My discomfort increased. The coffee must by now be very cold, I speculated. But the woman did not seem to notice.

I'd buy you another one, a hot one, I thought, but it would not end there. You would plan picnics. Read me out headlines. Tell me what your mother said.

The woman's sharp cobalt eyes flitted from one passenger to another. Surely they were not filling up with tears? I was grateful that momentarily she avoided mine. Hastily I searched in my briefcase for a book. For some reason I was fumbling. My hand trembled. The only book I could see was the thriller I had read on the downward journey that morning. I took it out.

She looked at me sharply. Did she know that I had finished it several stops before Liverpool Street?

Don't ask to borrow my book. It won't help you read my mind. There is a table between us carefully delineating our rights.

"I had to catch the four o'clock," she said, her voice very low, tremulous. Hard to catch what she was saying. Speak up, I said impatiently to myself, having a low tolerance of poor enunciation. Do not speak up, do not say anything at all, another voice warned. Too much is already being said.

"I had to catch the four o'clock," she said again, this time louder, looking earnestly at me. "I mean you can't keep staying in London. Not when it isn't your home."

There WERE tears in the blue eyes.

No-one took any notice of her. I was directly in line with the tearful questioning gaze. She had seen to that. She had marked me out. Perhaps she knew I always caught the four o'clock on Fridays. She had obviously been following my movements for weeks. Panic rose inside me. I forced myself to speak.

"London is an exciting city to work in," I said, trying to moderate my voice, hold the tone steady, knowing the other passengers were listening.

It was not a conversation. Surely she would not answer me. She would know better than to do that.

"After he went yesterday," she said, "I took the train to London. Thought it best. I couldn't think of anything else to do."

"Always the best," I said hopelessly. I could not think of anything else to say. I looked imploringly at the mother of the toddlers. She must understand. She must have neighbours like the woman in the pink silk dress. Could she not see I needed help?

"I went to the neighbour's first," the woman in liquorice pink silk said. "But they did not understand. They could not see I needed help. What could I do except to go to London?"

She put out her hand. Reached for mine.

I cannot touch you. I know the rules on trains. I have a Network card. South East region. Valid until next March. I've read the small print. Know the card is issued subject to the appropriate conditions. Know you have to keep within the Board's Conditions of Carriage for Passengers and Luggage. Know a passenger has to keep within the Excess Rules and Restrictions. Touching another passenger's hand, even one sitting opposite, sharing the same table, would be excessive, exceeding the limits. You do not spend ten pounds on a Network card and flaunt the regulations.

The hand that had clutched the plastic cup now clutched across the table at my hand. I was still grasping the thriller I had already read. The dénouement had occurred seven minutes before Liverpool Street. There had been plenty of time to gather my belongings together.

"I did not pack a bag," she said in a monotone. "I could not seem to gather my belongings together. You know how it is."

"I expect you have got relations in London," I said desperately. A shot in the dark.

She nodded. "Lil, the eldest." For a moment her voice became firmer. Her grip on my hand slackened. Then she shielded the blue eyes with her hand. "Lil always hated him. She would have been pleased he'd left. Good riddance she'd have said. Not your sort. Not your sort at all. Lil didn't much like me either. Too much like Mum I was. You know how it is in families. Think you can rely on them. Never works out. So I didn't go and see her. Not a lot of point. I just went and stayed as long as you can on the platform."

"Of course," I said.

"But they make you come home," she said in the same monotone.

"Of course," I repeated.

I looked around furiously. Was not anyone listening? Was it nobody else's responsibility? One man had put a Sony walkman in his ears. He was tapping his hands to the sounds.

"Best to go home," I heard a woman's voice saying. What a traitor you are I thought. How can you lie to her? But how can you tell the truth to her in a railway carriage? How can you tell it to yourself? Whatever you chose to tell, it would only be your truth.

My eyes reluctantly made it from the opened thriller to her face. I wanted to say: go on, tell me. I wanted to say: I am listening. I do care. I did not of course say anything. I managed a weak encouraging smile. She leant across to me, her fingers clenching mine as if they were plasticine.

"I don't know how to walk up the path to the front door," she said.

I wanted to say: would you like me to walk home with you? Walk up the front path. Take your key, open the front door. Go in. Read the paper while you put the kettle on. Tell you about my day, ask you about yours.

I wanted to say: would you like to borrow my company like one says would you like to borrow my book? Or my umbrella? I wanted to say it. But I said nothing. I knew it would not stop there. I told you earlier: Don't ask to borrow my book. It won't help you read my mind. Or make up yours. In any case I am not a lending library. I fear the rain. I have a life of my own. I did *want* to say it. So that not being a lending library is not the whole reason.

I do not know how to walk up the path to the front door with you, I thought. I have never done that for anyone.

I drew back my hand. Lowered my eyes to my book. I understand books. It is people that fluster me.

The passenger in the vulgar pink silk went on talking. Station after station. The four o'clock is the slow train. It stops everywhere. The man with the stereo in his ears turned the sound down. I did not know how to do that. Guiltily I envied him. Occasionally I looked out of the window. Looked and listened. Listened and looked. Flat landscape. Flat voice. Field after field. Station after station. I turned the pages to the dénouement. It lacked a certain surprise the second time around.

What will happen to you is a foregone conclusion. It would be rash to try and make changes. Field after field. Station after station. I watch the train pull in. I watch the train move off. Field after field. Station after station. The girl with the purple punky hair leaves it late. Leaps out suddenly. She is taking a risk. I never jump out when the train is moving. I am too old to change. Stops. Or my life. The guard called out "Whittlesford. Move into the first four carriages. It's a small platform." The regulars gave knowing smiles and moved imperturbably along the train.

"I live right at the top of Farmers Lane," she said. "Ever such a haul. I was thinking of sporting a cab." She sounded hesitant. "I've only got myself to think of now." The tears were pouring down her cheeks. Her skin was red and blotchy. A different shade of red from the streaky unkempt hair.

"Do that," I said. "Sport a cab."

I waited until she got off the train. I waited until everyone got off the train. Slowly I walked down the platform. Joe was on duty. "Your bike is alright miss. Kept a beady eye on it," he called out cheerfully. "You alright? You looked very upset this morning."

"Oh," I said, feeling suddenly caught out. "Funny that. This morning ... yes this morning ... I had forgotten about the bike. I thought I should have to sport a cab."

I cycled home, wondering how to walk up the path to the front door.

A SMALL NUMBER

There were just twenty people in the London gallery—a small number. Not many paintings either, by Charlotte Salomon, a young German artist. Well, she had been young when she painted them. They were wild, strange, bright: lots of blue, a great deal of red, some startling cadmium yellow, a small number of pigments that shone and battled.

The catalogue described her work as 'tri-coloured play with music'. The painter, it stated, used only three pigments. 'A small number' the catalogue said: just red, yellow and blue. Black had not been found.

Charlotte Salomon, it seems, was unusual in not using a greater number of colours. Why she used only three, confessed the catalogue writer, will remain her professional secret.

It probably will.

Charlotte Salomon died aged twenty-two in 1939—not a great number of years for a woman to help herself to a variety of colours. There were not a great number of women either, in Charlotte's family, and no-one else was a painter. All the women in Charlotte's family had killed themselves:

her mother had killed herself; her grandmother had killed herself. Two isn't that many, you could say: but two was all she had. Charlotte, the gallery guide told me, was always afraid she might do the same: kill herself.

She need not have worried. In the event she did not have to face that fear. The matter was taken out of her hands.

In 1939, when a great number of other women (and children and men) were facing their own fears, Charlotte was deported to the Auschwitz Women's Camp. She had just married one of a number of men she had been courting—a man called Alexander Nagler. On the day she left home she was five months pregnant. A small number of months, but enough to see a baby develop and live, had Charlotte stayed home and not taken any chances.

Charlotte was just one amongst a great number of women deported to Auschwitz that year. A large number were pregnant.

Charlotte was amongst the number (we don't know the number) who did not survive, did not come back, did not get to use black in her paintings, or purple or green or heliotrope.

A poet who was standing next to me in the gallery scribbled a poem about Charlotte Salomon's paintings. One verse ran:

> *Red yellow and blue*
> *These caught every relative*
> *And you.*

I'm not a poet but I wanted to write a story about Charlotte's life. There were not many months in her life—two hundred and sixty-four. A mere two hundred and sixty-four months lived in red, yellow and blue.

There was no further information about Charlotte Salomon, the painter: only that she had painted in three vivid tones—a woman, a young woman, who had used a small number of pigments.

I wondered what Charlotte's own number had been in the camp. I asked the poet. She had no idea. "Phone Auschwitz," she said. "They'll tell you her number."

Phone Auschwitz? I could not believe that anyone could pick up a public phone and dial Auschwitz—not on BT. I shall do it, I thought. I'll get Charlotte's number.

I did it.

I went to a phone, in a red box, outside the gallery—just red, not yellow, not blue. I got through to someone at Auschwitz. "I'd like Charlotte Salomon's number in the camp. 1939," I said. They put me on hold, then on to the Archives. I repeated my request. "Please send me a fax with your request," said a metal voice in the Auschwitz archives.

I faxed Auschwitz. Auschwitz faxed back. 'Dear Client, after research in our archives we wish to inform you that Alexander Nagler's registration number in the camp was 157166.' (Alexander Nagler, you may remember, was Charlotte's new husband, one of a large number of men who had courted her.)

'It is not possible', continued the fax, 'to establish Charlotte Salomon's number. It is very probable that she, being pregnant at the time, was selected to the gas chamber on her arrival, which happened in most such cases.'

There the fax ended. 157166 was the only number available. But it wasn't *her* number.

Charlotte, who I assume was selected (their word, their selection) out of a great number for the gas chamber, went into that chamber numberless: no number of her own.

I keep wondering about the red, yellow and blue. I discovered that cadmium yellow, Charlotte's particular shade, was named for a furnace used for smelting zinc.

You could say the colour was relevant.

But what about the black? No black has ever been found.

This story was written in appreciation of a poem and an account by Jane Liddell King. It was revised and performed at Hawthornden Castle during Sally Cline's 2003 Hawthornden Fellowship.

THE GREEN BIN

Daisy sat in the small green and white room. For the third time that day she picked up the exercise book that was to do as her diary. There was very little else to do in the small green and white room. Very slowly she started writing, trying to say some of the words aloud as she wrote them. She had a slight stammer. Soon she stopped trying to say them and wrote faster.

I am twenty-two years old, but I don't know their rules. Don't know how to get out of the bin. Ssh, mustn't let them hear me call their Centre that. They will punish me again if they hear the wrong words. I am here because I use the wrong words. Give them the wrong answers. Do not remember what they tell me.

No. No. Wrong again. I am in the Centre because I have symptoms. Because I am sick. I have symptoms because I am sick. Next time when I ask them they will let me out. Try it again slowly. All those of us who are sick have symptoms so that we may benevolently warn away those of us who are well. Yesterday, we who are sick, rang a warning bell. Today we have tidy sets of symptoms instead. Go away! Go away! Ring out the bells! Call out the symptoms!

Do not catch our plague! Save yourself from our diseases! If I wasn't sick I shouldn't have developed this stupid stammer. If I wasn't sick my words wouldn't stumble and limp along. My mind wouldn't dance on the ceiling. My brain wouldn't blind with nightmares. My throat wouldn't vomit these hideous sounds. I wouldn't smash into their green walls. I wouldn't shake when I think bad thoughts. I wouldn't shake when I look at their pictures. Grotesque pictures. Not like the pictures in my mind. Loving pictures of Faith and me. Stop it. Don't weaken. Don't think of Faith. All thoughts of Faith, my friend, my loving woman friend, are Bad Thoughts. They have said so. They have shown me pictures. Wrong, horribly wrong, pictures. But they do not believe me. And I cannot convince them. I can only shake. That's why I am in here.

Or am I here because of the crockery? Uncontrollable hatred of crockery. No-one else hates their crockery as I do. No-one else is afraid of it. Crockery that breaks as soon as I touch it. I can't stop these breakages. Not now. Can't stop the thoughts either. Not now. Pots break on their own. Mind cracks on its own now. Can't stop shivering. Hands shiver. Mouth shivers. They say it's because of the drinking. Drink and depression. More drinks to take away the depression. Clever thought that. More drink. Less depression. Worse work. Careful, be careful. My job is me. My job is what I have trained myself to be. My job is the me they respect. If you can't be a good mother you can be a good worker. If you are a good worker you won't be a good mother. I can't be a mother, good or bad. Women like me can't be mothers.

Concentrate on the job. Write the copy. Copy the writing. Mustn't sacrifice my job or I shall sacrifice the only self that is acceptable. Work means money. More drink means more money. Nigel starts to ration the money. My sensible husband is cautious with my money. Cautious with my drink. Advises me to be the same. It is my drink. My money. My depression. Try. Try. Try to remember. Oh yes, worse depressions because there's no money for drink and there's no doing without now. "Drink does help, Nigel," I remember explaining. "The shakes don't go away, but the bad thoughts do." Nigel is understanding. Sympathetic. Nigel thinks it is better if I go away. To this quiet place, this green painted Centre, where he says I won't have any more bad thoughts. I don't want to leave him. I don't want to trust Faith with him. "Trust me darling," Nigel says. "It will be alright." Does he know about the bad thoughts, my trusting young husband? Does he think my thoughts about Faith are bad? I can trust Faith, my loving friend, but I don't want to leave her. Don't want to leave little Faith either. Little Faith would have been two if she'd lived. Don't want to leave any of them. I love them so. Do they all think my thoughts are bad? Don't ask the men questions. Just provide the correct answers. Then they will let me out. They have told me. Bad thoughts. Concentrate. Bad thoughts. My thoughts are bad. Evil. Wicked. Sick. That's why I am in the cell. Not for drink or depression but for bad thinking!

I am here because I am sick. They have told both Nigel and I about this sickness. I hope it is not catching. I hope my healthy young husband will not catch it. It cannot be contagious or they would not let him come to see me every day. They do not let Faith come. Perhaps Faith could catch it. It would be selfish to give my sickness to Faith whom I love so deeply. Whom I long for. Don't say that. Don't write that. It is against their rules. They have invented the rules and they say they know about my sort. They are experts in my kind of sickness. This sickness they say *is* me.

I am sick with physical longing. Physical longing like mine is filthy. Diseased. I hear them whisper about it. They know about the longing to touch myself who is Faith who is a woman who is me. Soon they say I will have the correct physical repulsion at such a gross and indecent idea. They call it Aversion Therapy. I have only to wait quietly inside my cell, looking at their horrible pictures, repeat the right words, and wait for the Aversion Therapy to work. I must wait inside this clean white cell. My new bedroom. Wait silently. I must be silent if I cannot recall the correct phrase. Still and silent and locked up. Locked away from Faith who must never know, who must never be told, who must not be upset. Locked up daily waiting for my friend who does not come to see me. *My* friend Faith. No. Wrong again. Waiting daily for my nice young husband who visits daily. Nigel, my good looking husband, put me in here because he knows it is better for me. It is safer. Nigel has always seen to my safety. "Trust me, Daisy. It will be alright. I'll see that you're safe with me, Daisy." Clever of Nigel and the white-coated men to find a safe place to put the sick away. We have to be careful. The sick can contaminate the well.

When I was well and thought I was sick, before we were married, Nigel said: "You're certainly not sick, Daisy, for thinking you love two people. Any two people. Of course their sex doesn't matter. Sometimes I think the whole world is sick when it gives people ideas like that." It seems a long time ago he said that. Now I am sick and believe I am well and the rules have changed. Nigel has changed them. It is not the whole world which is sick, it is me for thinking I can love two people, one of whom is a woman. Now it is wrong to love. Wrong and sick. Sicker still to touch someone you love. But I never actually touched her. It is the truth and they will not believe me. Tell them again. Tell them now while they are not listening. Try once more to tell them the truth. More important, tell myself.

Tell myself I have never actually touched Faith. Faith, my loving teacher-friend. The teacher, nine years older than me, who learnt how to be a writer. Copy writer. Learnt from me. Copied from me. Copied. Learnt. Wrote. Succeeded. Now aloof and remote. Shut off from me as I am shut off from the rest of the world. The friend who taught me nearly everything I know about loving kindness. The kind of lovingness I grew crazy trying not to respond to. This *is* the truth I cry aloud in their cell. It is the truth that I never touched her, not in the sly seedy way they insinuate. Not in the grotesque way their pictures show. Sit still. Sit quite still in this small green and white cell and work out if this is accurate. Precise. Wait. They say I have a lot of waiting time in here to work things out. A lot of time before I can return to my job in the ad agency. Return to Faith. Little Faith or Big Faith? My head aches. Spins. Return to Faith and to my husband, who has always been Faith's friend too. To these two, who have been as my father and mother, brother and sister, my loving, careful, watching family.

No. I have never touched her like that. Nigel knows this. He has always known what I have felt. Always known what I have not done. Why doesn't Nigel tell them? Surely if it will help me to get out of here, Nigel should tell the men doctors. If he, my normal husband, tells them they will let me leave this place. Perhaps he will come today to tell them. I am sure he will come today. I wish I was as sure he will tell them. He says I must wait and trust. But some days I am not sure whom I can trust. I must wait. I have only to wait it out.

I am afraid sometimes to be with Faith. Afraid of what lies within myself. I am never afraid with Nigel. He keeps me warm. Safe. Makes me feel normal. Special to him yet like everyone else. Special woman. Ordinary woman. The woman who will become a good mother. In London after we move I subdue fears in the pace of my new job. I busy myself sparkling in the busy metropolitan advertising agency. Inside my head I am lonely for Faith because she too is preoccupied. Scared of her new job, a copy editor on a supermarket journal. Not the kind of writing we had in mind when we dreamed our hours away in her cold brick house in the northeast. She a teacher, I a student. But Faith is a realist, understands her own limitations. Her own capabilities. "I'm not a risk taker, Daisy. I'm not slick. My writing doesn't sparkle. I shouldn't suit a flashy advertising agency." She's right. She wouldn't. But "The Family Spinner" takes her on. Within six months of her careful steady hardworking start, they promote her. Give her a two year contract. Promote her again. She is still steady. Still hardworking. Still surprised at her success.

It never occurs to either of us that Faith will marry. She never does. Or that I will. It is Nigel's suggestion that Faith become my elder and only bridesmaid. We spend nearly a year in the flat before the Wedding. She is involved in her new job, has less time for me and mine. A few precious hours after work. We lie, lazy, close together. There is no rule about this. No penalties for loving her as I do. For wanting her as I do. Are there any penalties for desire? Do they see inside me to know and sanction what it is I desire so deeply. How can they judge? Nigel calls at the flat, this soft-keyed man I am to marry, not to spy or interrupt us, simply to settle with his books and papers, to share our quiet times. He is perceptive. Sensitive. Understands me. Stills the fears which lie below my noisy bubbling surface. Tries to make the new hustling life solid. He is my rock. He says

he will always be there. I want him more and more to leave
me alone with Faith. I do not know what I want. "Trust
me, Daisy," he says, "wait and see. You will change, adjust.
Once we're married it will be alright."

I cannot have what I want. Easier to want what I can
have. Marriage. Babies. Safer to want what they want me
to want. All of them. My father, my brothers, my man
friends. All of them. Even Nigel. He is not my lost brother,
the son my parents wished I was. He is not my friendly
man brother. He is my man friend. He prepares to be my
husband. Life After Marriage. My stomach is hollow at
the phrase. Marriage means babies. I want a baby. I want
love. I don't want to love Nigel to keep my baby. Life After
Marriage. Does he sense my mind is running away from
this blessed state? Will he run after me? Will he capture
my runaway mind? Does he feel in his body that mine has
already left to join Faith's? If he holds my body tighter
will that bring it back? Does he sense as he sits there with
us, stroking my hair, holding my hand, that my own hands
are already touching Faith's white breasts, already stroking
Faith's thighs, my finger already inside…inside…deep inside.
Stop. Draw back my secret hands. I have no right to put
my hands, my mouth, over her, into her, the way Nigel will
later by right put his hands, his mouth over me, into me. I
am as cold to his touch as I am warm to his words.

I want … What do I want? I want the secret places
he discovers dry in my loins to open up wet, melt into
the hidden places in Faith. I hunger to sink into her. To
feel her as I feel myself. Do not know how to. Scared
because I do not know how. More scared of finding out.
Need to find out. To find out with this woman, with some
woman, is to find myself. To know her is to know myself.
Perhaps for me it is the only way I can ever *be* myself.

Shocked again by that strange intensity. Want to diffuse it by telling it aloud. Fear blocks words. Cannot tell anyone. Not Faith. Not Nigel. Not friends. Not family. Tell them and I lose them. These are the unspoken rules. Tell them and I will lose him. Tell him and I will lose the chance of my baby. Don't tell him. Have the baby. Tell him. Lose the baby. Those are the rules. Tell Faith. Lose her. Tell Nigel, lose him. Cannot afford such losses. Cannot afford this secret madness. Crazed with this silent yearning. Someone must hear my words, whispering, someone must listen. Crazed. Crazy. Crazed. Crazy. Comes over me again in their cell. Crazed. Crazy. Put her away. Leave her alone. Keep her quiet. Keep her down. Shut her up. Shut her off. Crazed. Crazy. Crazed. Crazy. Quiet now. Still. Very still. Wait quite still until the words stop whirling and the shaking subsides. Don't say any more. It doesn't help. Words don't help. Don't say it. Don't think it. Don't remember it. Above all, don't do it. Leave the feelings. Then soon the feelings will leave me. The doctors assure me of that. Leave the feelings alone. Then they will leave me. Nigel promised me that after I told him. Told him and kept him. Kept him and lost myself. Lost the baby. Her bad feelings will leave. Her horrors. Her shakes. Her screams. Those dreadful screams I hear all the time. Her terrified screams when they come towards her with the needle. When they advance on her relentlessly with the pictures. Her silent noisy screams. They are terrible, her screams. The screams of the woman they say is inside me.

Stop her thoughts then her screams will stop. Leave the feelings. Don't act on the feelings. These are the rules. Men can act. Men are active. Women must not act. Or they must act only lies. Women must be passive. No action, passion instead. Commit only passion. No. No. Forget the passion.

That way the pain will go. But they can't lock you up for passion. Why then am I in the Green Bin if I didn't do it? Three years at university wanting to do it. Another year in the flat with Faith wanting to do it. A year of marriage, thinking about Faith, living with Nigel, still wanting to do it. Years, sick with wanting, with terrible need. The feelings which Nigel promised me would go away once we were married. Not his fault they didn't go away once we were married. He isn't in charge of my feelings. He is in charge of me. That is what is meant by Life After Marriage. If the feelings remain after marriage they are no longer right, they do not fit in with what is required of a good wife. Or a good mother. I want so much to be a good wife to my brother Nigel. Correction. I want so much to be a good sister to my husband Nigel. But the rules won't allow me. He has changed. He says the rules will help me. "A little conformity won't harm you, Daisy," he said with a laugh. "It's going to be alright. I love you. Keep trusting me then one day you too will love like this." I trust him more than I trust my own conscience. Think him better and wiser than I. Learn to respect him. Admire him. Be grateful to him. But never can my spirit, my body, learn to fall in love with this man. It has already fallen. It is faint with its fall. I forget my work. Forget to cook. To clean. To tidy. To get dressed properly. Even some days to wake up. Forget how to be a good wife. Would never have made a good mother. Wives and mothers get up regularly. Cook. Clean. They do more. I do less. Drink more. Lie in bed. Shake when I have to get up. Hide it from everyone.

The men who are my doctors, psychiatrists, editors, boyfriends, husbands, lovers, tell me wanting is sick. They all know me. The woman inside me is no longer hidden from these men.

I do not shake the Day of The Marriage. I have to trust
Nigel. I have hope for myself. But I do not look at my
bridesmaid. I cannot look at my bridesmaid who is the life
before marriage that I am giving up forever. For weeks
before the Day of The Marriage I want to tell her. So that
she will know it is not indifference to her which is making
me run out on our life. I never find the right words. I never
find any words. I am finding them now, I am writing them
now, many years too late, in the hope that someone reads
them, that someone tells her. At twenty-two I live close to
her but never tell her what I feel. Never again after that first
time talk to Nigel about it. Not until after The Marriage.
When I realised his wisdom has let me down.

I haven't changed. I haven't adjusted. I am the same.
But my world is different. There is no room in this new
married world for the old me. If I cannot change myself into
the new woman then I do not exist. I may be seen but not
recognised. Noticed but not accepted. I do what to me are
the usual things. And they say I am abnormal. I think what
to me are the regular thoughts. And they say I do not fit in.
I want what to me is natural and they say I am disturbed.
I think of Faith and know in my heart that I am whole. I
am well. I say it aloud, they tell me I am ill, label me sick.

One afternoon, in the kitchen, the new world and the
old me collide without warning. The explosion is terrifying.
When it subsides all the crockery is in pieces. My whole
body is shaking. There are pieces of me and my crockery
all over the floor. I am usually very tidy. It is extremely
disconcerting. When Nigel comes home he is very sweet to
me. Helps me to pick up the pieces of crockery. He knows
he cannot pick up the pieces of my old self. Somebody else
has to do that. I have a new and sudden stammer. I can't say
s or j. I can hardly talk to him. I listen as he says it isn't the

world which is sick but it is me. I cannot comprehend the meaning of those words. They are not like his other words. Not like them at all. The more I try and think it out the worse the stammer is, the fewer the words available. The greater his patience. He brings hot chocolate, puts his arms around me, phones the doctor. Nigel does all the right and proper things. He is understanding. He understands more than I do. He knows that I am confused, reassures me it will pass. He knows I am scared. He says he will wait for me. Why wait? Where am I going? Is he sending me somewhere? What have I done? Who are these white-coated men in my kitchen standing on my broken china? I am frightened. Very frightened. They have come to take me away.

There is no broken china here in my green cell. The white-coated men must have cleared away the last lot. They never seem to tire of their strange jobs. In this cold Green Bin I am still confused. Still scared. But Nigel says it will pass. The sickness that is. Nigel is a reasonable man. He is very respected by the white-coated men who pick up my china. The sickness will pass. He has told me. Whose sickness? I am muddled again. I no longer remember. My clever young husband has forgotten to tell me. He has failed me again. I start to stutter. They will ask me those questions again. He has failed to tell me the right answers. I wait anxiously for visiting hour. He will soon be here.

I fade away somewhere and I think I see Faith coming through the Centre's green and white gates. I watch her through my mind's window. The actual window in my cell is too high up, has too many bars for me to see out. There are no curtains to see through, a stammer and iron bars to inhibit me. Plenty of words but always the wrong ones. They do not talk to me at all. These white-coated men, who daily attend me, write up my file, take my pulse and my answers, mark them right or wrong in their notebooks. In this Centre they tell us nothing at all. Listen and smile and go on their way. I am just a patient. All patients are sick. All sick patients are ignorant, stupid, and inconsequential. Our function is to give no trouble. Our reward is to be ignored.

Suddenly I see Faith walking in through the cell door. She is grinning at me. Holding out her white hand. Her long fingers touch mine. I stop stammering. Full of words. Full of joy. I run to the cell door.

Wrong. Wrong. It isn't Faith. It isn't my friend. It is only an intruder nurse.

She isn't here, my friend, my loving woman friend. Remember, remember. They won't let her come here. Unjust. They won't tell her I am in here. Unjust! Unjust! Yell it in my head. Don't say it aloud. Because I know I will stutter. Unjust is a word with a j in it. I stumble over most words in this Centre, but specially those which contain j's and s's. There is a special white-coated linguist who thinks up those words to twist and confuse me. Remember. Remember. Nigel told me I cannot see Faith. Cannot see my friend. Not here, not now, not in this place. That would be wrong. Wrong and distressing. Whom would it distress? I keep forgetting. "Faith. It would be selfish to distress Faith. You know that Daisy."

Most of my ideas seem selfish viewed from outside this cell. I try hard not to be selfish. I want Faith to be my friend when I come out. If I come out. How many more visiting hours before they let me out? I find visiting hours tedious. Very few people come and see me in the neatly allotted times.

Each day I get myself tidy. Brush up my replies. Wait cheerfully. Then nobody comes. It isn't at all like a regular hospital. No grapes. No visitors. Perhaps grapes and visitors are out of season.

Or perhaps my family and friends live a long way from The Bellham. Strange that I don't know my own label but I do know the Centre's. "This used to be an asylum called The Bedlam," a nurse told me cheerfully. "You were drugged when he brought you in."

I am glad we don't have asylums today in England. The English are extremely advanced. They have invented these pleasing clean Centres where you can learn to do basketwork, weaving and embroidery if you are a girl, and woodwork and metalwork if you are a boy. The Centres are where they read you the rules and teach you the right answers and make everything refreshingly simple. It should be easy to get out of a Centre.

I want to do metalwork. I want to be purposeful. I shall tell them today. My purpose is to make bookends. Want to touch smooth metal bookends. We are allowed the small number of books which fit tidily on the green and white painted bedside cupboard. I read my five books, the five books they allowed me, soon after I got here. I ask Nigel for more. He brought me five more. He tried to take away the first five. I argued. I struggled. I wanted the first five. They remind me of home. You are allowed to have any number of possessions about you at home. He left me the first five, but wasn't pleased with me. I had too many books. They toppled all over the tidy green cupboard. The nurses were furious. I stacked them up again. Quite neatly. The nurses were cross. It isn't allowed. Didn't I know that? The white-coated doctors sent them home in a parcel. Plain brown wrapping. No-one could possibly tell if they were the books I wasn't allowed. I still want more books. Begged Nigel to bring some more. Perhaps he will bring them in the visiting hour.

It is Visiting Hour now. I am terribly neat. My hair is pulled into bunches. They say long hair like mine is messy.

Untidy. I am scared they will cut it. Nigel thought up the
bunches. I am ready. I'm waiting. The nurse is opening my
cell door. I shall please her. I have the right words today. Tell
her I know who I am waiting for. My kind young husband.

The nurse is alone. There is nobody with her. She says
Nigel won't be coming today. Is he ill? Is he working? He
comes every day. The panic is starting. The words are tumbling
over themselves. Find others. Be careful. Choose clear words.
Ask her again. Try it slower. Don't hurry. Nigel must be ill.
He must be working. He *will* come. He *must* come.

The doctors don't think any more visitors are sensible.
They advise complete isolation. A good rest is what is wanted.
Visits excite me. Nigel, says the nurse, agrees with the doctors.
He won't be coming for a while. He thinks it best. He wants
me to recover. The nurse tells me to relax for an hour and
then she will take me to Occupational Therapy. To continue
my needlework. Nigel isn't coming to see me. No-one ever
comes to see me. No-one else seems to know I am here.
Nigel will not bring my books. I want to see Nigel. I want to
see *someone*. I want something to read. I cannot relax. Careful,
must try and relax. Think about the books. Know that more
books will mess up my room. Mess up my clean cell.

I tidied my cell especially for visiting hours. Now no-one
will see it. Mustn't mess up their cell with a lot of new books.
Mustn't mess up their rules with a lot of untidy reading.

But what if I made bookends? That is the answer. Think
about that. Fasten on that. Bookends are safe to think
about. There's no rule about bookends. Then I can ask for
my books. That will be a reasonable request. I know several
boys in this centre who have made hard metal bookends.
They gave theirs away, as presents to visitors. I shan't do that.

Perhaps if I worked hard at Occupational Therapy I could
even make a bookcase. I want to build a bookcase. I want

to build something. Something big and strong and sensible. I want to build a whole bookcase and then ask to have my books in here, so that I can go away, far away, into my books. I want to do woodwork as well as metalwork. I shall tell them in Occupational Therapy.

It is time. It is time. I am hot with excitement. I ask the Occupational Therapist when she hands out dozens of skeins of coloured embroidery silks. I tangle them up in excitement awaiting her answer.

She is angry with me for wanting to go with the boys. For wanting to be like a boy. I don't want to be like a boy. I just want to make metal bookends and a wooden bookcase. "You'll never get better, dear, as long as you have ideas like that," she says firmly. "Now, here are some lovely new cottons. Start again. Try something constructive."

She walks over to the man in the white coat at the end of the room. Daisy is still very sick, doctor," she says. "She is also becoming increasingly rebellious. We are going to have to take a firm line. What I recommend is …"

I stop listening. But someone is talking. Daisy is still very sick, doctor. The person talking is clambering in my head. Fighting with someone behind my eyes. Is inside my head. Talking inside my head. Daisy is still very sick. Who let the person inside? Still very sick. Very sick. Sick. Sick. There are two people talking. Shouting. Sick. Still very sick. Yes, she is. Sick. Very sick. I wish they would stop it. Why doesn't someone stop them? The sounds are too loud in my ears. If they aren't careful they will burst through my eardrums. Isn't she sick?

How can I make my silks into a bookcase when people are shouting in my ears? Shouting inside my head. Concentrate. Knot the coloured silks together. Tight together. Tight together. Still very sick doctor. Tight together. Still very sick.

More coloured silks. Tighten knots. Block out their sounds
with my coloured skeins. Sick doctor. Still sick doctor.
We are going to have to take a firm line. Firm line. Firm
line. I cannot see the colours of my silk bookcase because
of the noise in my ears. All my silks are coloured green.
Green is the colour of my cell. Green is the colour of my
blood. Green is my sickness. Tight together. Concentrate
on pulling them tight. The rope is beginning. Tighten the
rope. Put the rope around my neck. Sick doctor. Still sick.
What I recommend is… What I recommend is. Make sure
the books can't slip. Neck can't slip.

Sick. Still sick. Stop the voices. Pull the rope. They are
coming towards me. They'll take me away. Finish my bookcase,
before they get me. Finish the rope. Finish. Finish. Hurry.
Hurry. Pull the silk together. Hold my neck steady. Now
for the knot. Stop those voices. Sicker. She's getting sicker.
Louder. It's getting louder. Pull it tight. Pull it tighter. Tighter.

"I've got her. Hold her hands down. Where's the needle?
Hurry, nurse. Sharp now. Over there. That's the way." The
ice cold instructions issue from the man in the white coat.

I am crying inside because I know that I cannot have
my books now. They will not let me have anything now. I
cannot climb out yet. They have broken my rope. I broke
their rules again. Now they will break me.

Someone plunges in the needles. The woman screams.
I am the only one that hears her.

"Ok, ok, everyone. It's over now. Settle down everyone.
Take her back to the ward, nurse."

★ ★ ★ ★

Daisy put down the exercise book. It was a few minutes to
Visiting Hour. She tied her hair neatly into bunches.

DAISY WRITING LETTERS

W rite me letters. (You say.) Your letters are beautiful. I can show them to anyone. Of course I don't, you add hastily. I know they are intimate. But they are letters of which I can be proud. Letters are allowed.

You drift off into an embarrassed silence.

Letters are allowed I say angrily to myself, wondering what else your husband allows and disallows.

But I do not stop writing.

I write you letters. Send them urgent. Special delivery. An extra two dollars. To show importance. Wing emotion. Make my mark.

Fill a void.

Your morning mail comes heavily stamped with my feelings. (Can he tell? Does he read them?) While you, a void, showing yours.

Here there is no-one but me to read the male. For by now I am more obsessed with him than with you. Your letters to me have become his letters to me. He, it seems, makes allowances. (Letters are allowed.) What else will he allow? I scratch danger with my pen nib.

Letters are allowed. Letters reach the edge. But they cannot topple your heart into warm pits. Warm and waiting. Lazily you still send yours second class.

Letters are allowed. They cannot spill this wet and jerky wanting. My fingers parting your wetness leave no trace across the typed page.

Strange. Because the keys are still slightly moist...

RETURN MATCH

T he tube pulled in competently to Maida Vale station. It was twenty-nine years and three months since she had last been there. Few underground stations had left her with such chilling recollections. She shivered slightly and pulled her mohair wrap more tightly around her. It was June and she had not thought to bring a coat.

Daisy had almost forgotten what it was like travelling on a tube away from the fever of the city to the shallow reaches of the suburbs, a tiring journey she had excitedly made twice a day, every day, during her early life as an eager young London journalist.

Daisy did not find much to excite her nowadays, although her assignments, world-wide and well paid, brought her a good living and a high degree of recognition. For the last twelve years she had resided abroad, faxing her weekly "Letter from South Africa," "Letter from the Gulf", "Letter from Israel" or from wherever she had taken up temporary professional residence, to whichever English newspaper offered her the highest rate and the most compelling by-line.

Occasionally strangers, never her friends, would say to her: "Do you miss not having a family?" Systematically and consistently Daisy would reply pleasantly: "No, not at all. I am thoroughly immersed in my work. I play a lot of sport. Children might have been interesting but a dreadful interruption."

The train doors rolled smartly open. For a moment Daisy hesitated. Could she face the memories outside the doors? She laughed at herself. In her work, she had faced wars, atrocities, violence on a scale that tore apart her descriptive powers. What after all were a few memories? She gripped her briefcase and walked with determination through the station, where used tickets, discarded by casual passengers blew about in the breeze.

After walking briskly for five minutes, she found herself once more at the corner where Elgin Avenue turns into the little side road that houses a set of unfashionable but sturdily built red and grey stone flats. No 75 was in the basement, at the end of a flight of crumbling steps. As a young girl she had felt this, a basement lifestyle, to be somehow trendy, a mite improper, admittedly a *dank* place but one in which a cool young reporter ought to live. The steps were still crumbling, the air still felt dank.

A young woman with a baby in one hand, heaving a buggy clumsily in the other, was climbing up. They were almost face to face. "Are you looking for anyone?" she asked Daisy, smiling and gasping with the effort of handling buggy and baby simultaneously.

"I don't think so…I'm not sure," Daisy said, not moving out of the woman's way. The woman looked at her curiously then assembled the child inside the stroller and trotted off, keeping up a running patter of friendly one-sided chitchat as she walked.

Daisy sat down on the top step and looked around. "They have taken away the tennis courts," she said out loud and realised she wanted to cry. There had always been tennis courts outside the flat. They had always promised each other that when they had a few spare hours they would learn to play well.

* * * *

"I haven't got time for a game tonight darling," Nigel had called out. He was busy packing up his books. "I'm due back at College, a couple of meetings; maybe we can get a game in next weekend when you come up. How about that?"

Dear patient, painstaking Nigel, always concerned for her welfare, always sad about leaving her when it was time for him to go back to Oxford, where he was now a modest academic, instead of the lively newspaper editor she had met and married.

"Sounds good to me," she called back. She went into their tiny muddled study and hugged him as he sat on the floor carefully separating which books he could not do without from those he could afford to leave behind. When he was most immersed in his work, he would push his tortoiseshell spectacles off his eyes and lodge them in his curly black hair. There they were, as usual, in that ridiculous position. She took them off and waved them in front of his eyes. "You'll get eyestrain peering at those musty old books," she said fondly.

Daisy was proud of him, proud of herself, proud of the money she had earned as a journalist so that he could study while she worked. She enjoyed racing around Fleet Street aping the older and only marginally calmer news writers. Sometimes she was lonely but she made do. Nigel, now that he had finished studying, was on the Faculty, was content and purposeful, relaxed. Nigel, as far as Daisy was concerned, was safe and away. She visited him regularly every weekend, bouncing into his quiet and moderate book lined life with outrageous treats and appalling tales of her excessive behaviour. She did not however tell him everything. Daisy felt safe because Nigel trusted and cherished her.

"We need to talk about starting a family, about you leaving Fleet Street, joining me in Oxford," he would say most weekends. They would laugh and plan, then break up conversation for tennis or drinks. The weekend, on which Daisy depended for repose and stability, would end, and they would continue their separate lives.

Weekends were when Daisy recovered from her job, recovered small fragments of herself. During the weekdays she poured her time and energies into journalism. Bad news was good news. She thrived on public disasters. Being first on the scene was everything. She seldom questioned the value of what she did, and was careful not to discuss it too fully with Nigel who nowadays questioned everything.

Some of herself she saved. Put it away carefully for lunch hours or evenings. There were secret lunches and suppers saved for Bodie. She always thought of him by his surname. A distancing process. It was important to distance the man from himself. In the early days, when Nigel had still been in Fleet Street, Bodie had been his friend, a junior colleague, on The Daily Globe, where Nigel had been Night Editor before he went to Oxford.

"Good man, Bodie," Nigel used to say to her. "Some people despise him for not being one of the head-types, he's certainly not an intellectual, but he's a very shrewd bloke. Got good judgement in political matters. Careful type. He'll lead one of our papers one day. You'll see."

Daisy smiled when Nigel talked about Bodie. No Bodie was not a head person. Not a head person at all. Bodie was a body person. His body and hers were good together. He had been surprisingly shy at first. Nigel was right. Bodie's head was stubbornly conventional. No radical intellect. Bulky physique. Strong arms. One night after a discreet dinner at No 75, (Daisy loved the danger of eating there, Bodie hated it) he said to her: "You think I am square, cautious, don't you?" Daisy could hardly have disagreed. Bodie was indeed the careful type. Careful not to let anyone know how he felt about her. Nobody who mattered, nobody at work. It was work, not feelings, which were critical to Bodie.

Suddenly he was promoted. He left the Daily Globe, moved on, moved up, moved away. He became the senior roving reporter for The Daily Circus, Britain's largest circulation popular paper. (Ten years later Nigel was again to be proved right when Bodie successfully led The Scottish Daily Circus through its greatest crisis period.)

After months of seeing his big burly figure around Fleet Street's pubs and offices, Daisy was suddenly left with only his smug-looking photo which appeared above his daily by-line from Singapore. She looked at it and tried to recall his large gentle hands on her body. He had never been the tough aggressor his physique might have suggested. He had been soft spoken with a slow firm touch.

"Bodie is a good man, Daisy," Nigel had said about his friend when she had been reluctant to invite him to one of their supper parties. "Worth getting to know. Try him out. See what you think."

A good man. By Fleet Street standards. A hesitant man by any standards. He hesitated a full three weeks before he allowed his friend and senior colleague's wife to try him out. He never told anyone. The careful type. That in itself was so rare in rumour ridden Fleet Street that Daisy might almost be forgiven for believing he was possessed of integrity. Ten years later when he edited and led his paper through its most turbulent times she realised bitterly he had been awash with caution not integrity. Bodie was a fine political animal. A careful political animal. It was not Daisy's face or position he was saving by not telling.

Now he was due back. He had not however told anyone he had asked for three days leave. He had not told anyone about the baby. He was a clean living cautious animal. He would fly cautiously back from Singapore to London. He would spend three days in England. Three days in which to find £300 and the finest butcher. Then he would have to fly back. Roving reporters have to return to base after accomplishing any mission. He had a *real* job to perform out there in the Middle East. She was lucky he had managed to find time to come home at all.

He called her from the airport. "Let us not meet at your place. I do not think that would be safe. I know Nigel is not at home, dear, but it still would not be very nice to stay there. Not tonight. Got to think of the old etiquette eh? I have booked us a room in a hotel. It is a quiet little place in Bloomsbury. Virginia Woolf territory. You'll like that."

Not an intellectual. But thoughtful to recall her preferences at a time like this.

"You are alright aren't you, Daisy?" he remembered to ask. "Not been in any trouble or anything?"

"No trouble," she was curt. "Yes I am alright. Yes I shall meet you at the hotel. No I do not want to take a taxi. I shall drive my car."

She had never remembered the name of that hotel. She had never forgotten the look of that room. Old fashioned, once ornate, with dingy dark green woodwork, almost slime coloured, mottled cream wallpaper, slightly peeling where it met the window sill, huge brownish furniture, not much of it, just a mammoth wardrobe and an old chest of drawers and dressing table with a mirror which had come off its stand and had to be propped up. It did not matter that there was so little in the room, they were not staying long.

"Just one night in this jolly old tub," Bodie said, patting it and her alternately. He sounded less sure of himself than he did in his columns from Singapore. His face looked less smug; it wore a slightly anxious look. "One jolly night and then we shall be away," he said as if to reassure himself. He appeared to have forgotten Daisy was with him.

The jolly old tub was a vast brown wooden bed with a vulgar scarlet satin bedspread draped over it. Virginia Woolf would have despised it. It was, however, as Bodie said, only for one night, and one could not be choosy. It was after all extremely quiet. Only a cemetery in Central London would have been quieter.

There was not much to do that night, and little to discuss, so they went to bed early. About eight thirty-five. Bodie had supper first. Daisy refrained. She had twice been sick. Bodie was exhausted after his flight, but was as always considerate. "You don't sound too good. I'm a bit jet lagged myself. I don't expect you want to make love, do you dear? Let's just cuddle up, shall we?" Before she could think of an appropriate reply he had cuddled up under the vulgar scarlet satin cover, his large hands stretched above his head on the alien hotel bolster. He slept long and well.

She stared above her at some faded cream angels embossed on the wallpaper ceiling. She had not noticed them earlier. She stayed awake for ten hours and fifteen minutes and managed to impress on her mind, for all time, every detail of the slime green and cream hotel room.

In the morning he was frighteningly efficient. Checked them out of the Bloomsbury Hotel. Into a cab. Over to a bank. Then to a second. Then to a third. "You cannot be too careful when you want to withdraw cash," he had intoned. A final cab took him to Harley Street. She made her way back to the hotel to pick up her car. She had recently cleaned and polished her beloved bright blue-green mini. The paintwork glistened. Then she drove very slowly to Harley Street.

Bodie had arrived, was impatient, somewhat flustered. The butcher was waiting for them in his silky green curtained waiting room. She stepped gingerly on what looked like green velvet grass. Bodie and the butcher made small talk. She said nothing. She waited for the man who had been her lover to remind the butcher about the anaesthetic. Bodie said nothing. Bodie had forgotten. "Tell him darling, tell him." She had found her voice. Or someone's voice…Fear was making the voice scream. The sound was shocking in the gentle green blood palace. "Tell him, you promised me. You promised me you would tell him. You promised you would tell him I shan't be able to stand the pain." Her voice rose.

Bodie stood up. His big body loomed over her. She shrank back from it. She stopped screaming, she did not try to talk. Tears ran down her face. "Stop it. You must trust the gynaecologist. He knows what he is doing, darling." Her lover was very angry. He was a person who abhorred fuss of any kind. Shunned confrontation as he would disease.

"Please agree to do it our way, Mrs er um Bodie," the smiling specialist said. "It is the time factor you see. I have explained everything to your, ah er um, to Mr Bodie. We simply cannot give general anaesthetics to all our ladies and

still guarantee to get them out for their next appointment
on time. Our dear ladies, like ourselves, like yourself indeed
dear Mrs ah er um Bodie, lead such terribly busy lives."

Her tears were messing up the green velvet grass. She
trod in her tears so that they did not show. The butcher was
still talking or sharpening the blades, one or the other. "My
dear Mrs Bodie, believe me there is nothing to worry about.
We do, after all, know our job." He laughed deprecatingly.
Bodie nodded as if satisfied. "It is only a minor repair job
after all. Hardly needs a general now does it? We just give
you a lovely dreamy pill and you won't notice anything.
Isn't that so Mr Bodie?"

Bodie looked a trifle uncomfortable. "Tell him, for God's
sake, tell him," she screamed. "I shan't be able to stand it."
She began to run from the green velvet room. He strode
after her and leant against the waiting room door. "Daisy
STOP THAT! You are getting hysterical." He placed his big
arm around her, and held her stiffly for a few seconds. He
waited until she had somewhat calmed down then walked
back to the specialist, who was still patiently smiling, and
began to count out the money.

She edged nearer the door. Crying and gasping. Either
Bodie or the butcher stopped her. It did not matter which.
By then they were the men between her legs.

The man who had been her lover had left the green
carpeted blood palace. She was alone in a room with
eight or nine other women. They were on their own too.
Obviously this was not a place for men. Some women came
in with men. They all left without them.

The secretary-nurse woman was staring at her. How odd,
Daisy thought. She was not there so the secretary-nurse
could not possibly see her. The woman said curtly "Follow
me downstairs." She followed her down two flights of stairs

through a room with three little beds, and then into a large
white surgery.

There was a big stainless steel bin just inside the room.
Protruding from it was a black plastic rubbish bag. As she
stumbled past it, she glanced in. The secretary-nurse said
sharply: "Don't look in there. The last girl was stupid. Far
too far gone. There is no point in looking."

She was too late to stop Daisy. Inside the black rubbish
bag was a mess of flesh. Like assorted amputated knees.
The top lump was very large. Different from the rest.
Recognisably shaped. It was NOT like a baby. She had
seen babies. They were fat and round and stupid. They were
red and wizened and alive.

This was more like a grotesque miniature old man. This
was also stupid. This was also red. Very red. Very wizened.
This was not alive. This was not a baby.

She wanted to run but she could not move. She was
sick all over the specialist's expensive green pile carpet. The
vomit was green pile too. Daisy wondered idly about mix-
and-match.

The icy nurse-woman was furious. She shovelled up the
vomit and put it in the same black plastic bag that contained
the flesh.

Then she said sharply to the man-doctor: "She has
brought up her dream pill, doctor. Is there time to give
her another?"

His voice was smooth and luxuriant like his salon. "Of
course not," the silky tone purred. "We are running ten
minutes late already. We all know the rules. We must not keep
our ladies waiting, any more than they must keep us waiting."
Then sharply, the purr cut off: "Get her in the chair nurse."

Daisy wondered idly why he did not talk to *her*. She
supposed it was because she was no longer there. The chair

was padded leather with a frame of steel like the rubbish bin holder and the nurse-woman's eyes. She knew she must not sit in the chair. Too late she started to fight people in the room. There seemed to be a great number of people, all of them with magnified legs and arms, holding down her legs, holding down her arms. One of them held on to her body and fastened it in to the steel rimmed chair. Another held her legs. Someone, was it the doctor, was it the nurse, pushed her legs down, strapped her more tightly into the seat, pulled her feet up in front of her into some kind of harness.

The nurse-woman picked up two shiny instruments and handed one to the doctor. No wonder Bodie had brought her here. He was a careful man who needed to place her in the hands of other careful men.

Suddenly she heard someone scream. It was someone near her, for the screams were loud, loud and terrible. The nurse-woman carefully handed the man the second shiny instrument. It looked like a knife.

The woman was screaming again. Daisy was sure it *was* a woman. Only a woman would be so stupid as to break the peace of this expensive salon, with such loud and dreadful screams. Daisy was sure they would punish the woman.

She stopped thinking. She was nearly knocked off the chair by a sharp slap across the face. "STOP that screaming. Sit STILL. How can the doctor work properly if you do not sit still and be quiet?"

The nurse-woman was being very reasonable. She, it seems, was not being reasonable. Some man had paid her money. She must take his choice. If that other woman's screams were hers, then that other woman's pain must be hers. It must be her that they are punishing. She tells the other woman, who may be her, but there is no accurate way of knowing, to be quiet, so that the man-doctor can work

properly. Ten minutes or a life later, she was outside the
room, lying next door in the place with three single beds. All
the beds had pale green bedspreads. The floor was covered
in more thick green carpet. One woman was just waking up.

Her cheeks were tinged a putrid pale green, the same
colour as the counterpane and the floor covering. A second
woman was slowly getting dressed. Her arms were moving
stiffly as if they did not belong to her: "Hurry up, your taxi
is here". The woman quickened her pace obediently and
was slightly sick on the bed. She did not appear to notice.
Daisy watched her move like a well-dressed puppet to the
door. The woman did not look at her, but Daisy thought she
knew what she was feeling. She must be worrying about the
cab. Taxis were always a luxury. Hurry, she said to herself
or to the woman. We must not keep the taxi men waiting.

Half an hour later she had left the salon, and found
herself standing by her battered blue mini. There were new
scratches on her once shiny turquoise paint. Sadly she put
an affectionate hand on the car's bonnet. Then very slowly
she heaved herself inside. She drove in first gear down the
length of Harley Street. Blood began soak through the
sanitary towel onto the clutch pedal.

The butcher, thinkingly, had put a coil in the massacred
body that was again hers. "We do not want a repeat
performance now, do we?" he had purred before she left.

It took her an hour in the traffic to reach Maida Vale. She
was nearly home. She turned into Elgin Avenue and began
to drive faster. Suddenly a dog slipped its leash and raced
into the road in front of her car. Her reactions were less
alert than usual. At another time she might have swerved
and missed it. This time she was not able to miss it.

She stopped the car after she had run over the dog. She
was a few minutes away from the flat. She looked ahead

and in the distance she saw that there were couples playing tennis on the courts. She supposed she might never play tennis again. The dog's owner was hysterical with grief and anger. "You and your crazy driving! Look what you have done. You murderess. You murderess!" She screamed and screamed at Daisy who sat silently staring ahead at the couples in bright white shorts waving rackets and running cheerfully across the court. Daisy hoped the woman would not shake her. Silently she picked up the woman's dog and put it in the back seat of her car. The dog's blood began to seep onto the clean back seat.

She knew what she had to do. She knew you had to report an accident to a dog. She motioned to the woman to get into the passenger seat, then drove the woman and her dog to Maida Vale police station. She parked the battered turquoise mini. Her blood had dried and clotted on the clutch pedal.

After the interview at the police station, she walked past her car, and went on walking until she reached the underground. Slowly she entered Maida Vale station.

★ ★ ★ ★

Daisy had cramp in her left leg. It had been bent under her as she had sat on the top of the steps for several hours. She rose awkwardly to her feet, and looked across at the block of flats which had been erected where the tennis courts used to be. They looked grey and sombre in the half light. She was sorry they had never learnt to play tennis well. She did however still knock the ball around wherever she happened to find a court.

She glanced at her watch. There was just time to get to the shop which was restringing her racket. She closed her eyes momentarily as she walked into the station. She did not remember the journey to the shop but there she was inside. The salesman efficiently produced her racket.

"Here you are. It was only a minor repair job after all."

THE THOUGHT OF YOU

I thought the thought of you would be enough. Having had you … An unsound phrase … Just the once. Quite sufficient. "We must not make commitments." You said that in a trice. Now imagination will suffice.

I thought the thought of you would be enough. Having seen you…with…as they say…the naked eye. Spilling over my naked, shaking self. Not once but twice. Now imagination must suffice.

I thought the thought of you would be enough. I have your photo, I've read your card. I have carefully reduced the risk of attaching value, or setting any price, on… Imagination WILL suffice.

I thought the thought of you would be enough. I thought we might try and turn it into Good Solid Friendship. I thought ….

Screw thinking! It's you I want.

RECENT CHANGES AT A CANADIAN UNIVERSITY

I had been away from Nova Scotia. Had travelled to Europe, then to the USA. I had not seen him for several years. The last time was at their rundown farm in the country outside Halifax. He had long uncombed hair knotted back in a plait. They kept chickens and a goat. He wasn't making money and he wasn't making his wife happy. Nor was the countryside. She was a city girl.

He wanted to be an academic, he said. She encouraged him. Brought him books. Helped with his research. Fed the chickens. Fed him.

I left them to it.

Then eight years after that meeting I was invited to speak at an East Coast University.

I hardly recognised him. What is it I ask myself? What has happened I ask him? He no longer wears a plait. He no longer keeps chickens. The way the Radicals can. He is no longer the same person. Or man. Now he wears short hair. Now he is a Chairperson or Man. Runs a Department instead of his wife. It is certainly a new life.

She runs loose with no shoes on. The way Radical Wives can. She does not look quite the same person. She does not

act quite according to plan. He encourages her freedom.
Admires her aplomb. (He calls her Mom.) He buys her
new shoes. He finds she has outgrown them. And him.
He thinks it a whim.

Then he discovers she has discovered another life.
He discovers she has discovered another Radical Wife.

He tells me he wishes they still kept chickens.

SWEET ADELINE

D aisy comes to, slowly. Something is throbbing. She turns her neck slightly on the pillow.
Christ!

A searing pain releases a word which as a Jew, even one who doesn't go to synagogue, and the wife of Jerry Angel, who occasionally does, rarely uses.

Jerry (named for the Hebrew prophet Jeremiah) was sufficiently well known within the Jewish community, mainly for his spellbinding music, to refrain from the more obvious of Gentile expressions.

As a New Yorker, marginally converted to the less frenzied life of an English countryside, he basked in the appreciation the British gave his talents.

On his inconsistent visits to his wife and daughter, Deborah, residing in a quiet Sussex village (Jerry of course has a London apartment which houses his main studio) Jerry has been known to don a deerstalker for public appearances at the wheels of his classic car Adeline. He was spotted sporting a bowler for fun at a session in the recording studios which the media attended. The press regard his occasionally uncharacteristic clothes as eccentric and obediently take photos.

Today Jerry is conspicuously absent from Daisy's re-emergence into a ragged form of life.

Pain pulls at her forehead. She winces. Lie still, she instructs herself, lie still. Oh dear Mother of God, this time the pain is treacherous. Not even Jerry's music to which despite their rows and difficulties she is still addicted could lessen the pain or momentarily distract her. Daisy's desire is for independence, to be seen as a woman separate from the public image of Jerry Angel's wife, and from the private myth, (Jerry's personal controlling myth) of Daisy as the conventional Jewish help meet.

That she is not.

Jerry would quote from the Bible: "And the Lord God said it is not good that the man should be alone; I will make a help meet for him."

At the start of their marriage, she had believed that. If he had left some part of her to grow and develop, if he had not entirely taken her over, she might have been the partner required by Genesis 2 verse 18.

The conflict between what she might have been, left to herself, (which *he* will not) and what he insists she become, (which *she* will not) has modified her once stormy behaviour. On their good days she is still passionately under his sway.

"Now you're thinking straight, honey!" he approves.

On their bad days she remains resentful and stubborn.

"Melt, honey, melt!' he persuades.

Recently, Daisy, once outspoken and articulate, has started to stammer under the stress.

To speak now would result in a stammer. She is sure of that. Speaking, however, appears impossible due to the buzz of noise inside her head. Is the buzz inside or outside her head? There is a black splinter inside, tearing at her edges. Certainly there is a sawing sound inside, but the buzz is somewhere in her room. Something does not feel right about her room. People's voices reach her. A cacophony of low cheerful sounds. Metallic talk. Then tapping. Tap tap. Tap tap. Brisk footsteps approach. Tap tap. Then the sounds stop.

"She is coming round now."

A clear tinkly voice. Like a delicate cup touching a fragile china saucer. The white Coalport cup and saucer with the single red rose inside the rim, which Jerry had given her one Chanukah. Along with the engraved silver Menorah.

"That china could only be British!" Jerry had enthused.

The candelabra was to celebrate their eighth Chanukah together.

"How could I not give you a Menorah? One silver branch for each of our eight years. After the next eight years, honey, I'll get you golden."

How could she resist his enthusiasm, and later his ardour? Together they lit one light on the first night of the Festival, two the following night, until on the last night they all shone together. They took the candelabra with them into the bedroom.

Daisy, taken in by silver candles and a golden glow, had hoped that they would spend the remainder of the holidays together. Their daughter, Deborah, would be home from school and in Daisy's view needed more of her father's time and attention. Deborah, named by Jerry from the Bible for a prophetess, was a feisty young woman.

"Hardly surprising," Jerry would say proudly. "Remember, honey, Deborah was a Judge. Pretty smart woman."

Daisy recalled that Deborah dwelt under the palm trees of her name, and when the Lord God of Israel commanded her, she took ten thousand men to Mount Tabor and ensured that the enemy, at that time the King of Canaan, was delivered into the hands of the woman.

Yes, Jerry was keen on judgements as long as they were in his favour. He approved fierceness in women as long as they did not cross his particular path.

"You should stay for the holidays, Jerry," Daisy had said firmly.

The following day, equally firmly, Jerry left to take Adeline, his classic car, to a rally in Paris. The Jewish Holidays were over. Biblical injunctions forgotten.

"Can't say when I'll be back sweetie. You know how it is."

She knew how it was.

But mistakenly she argued with him.

By then Daisy was used to Jerry's rants, his sudden rages, his abject apologies.

"I cannot think how it happened. I wouldn't have had it happen for the world. Sometimes I think I am going crazy with these rages. You know how it is honey?"

She knew how it was.

What she did not know now, as she lay shakily in bed, was what had happened to her the day of the car race or why she was here. Or even where 'here' was. Shooting pains made concentration a challenge, but she began to listen intently.

"She is stirring."

The voice has become brisker, like the footsteps. Whose brisk voice in her bedroom? She tries to open her eyes but as she does so the buzz starts up again. The mild throbbing changes to thunder. Her left eyelash brushes against something scratchy, something around her head. There is a new burning sensation.

Close that eye she tells herself. In the constant absence of another adult she has become used to talking to herself. Struggle with the other one, she encourages. Through a veil of discomfort she manages to focus on another bed on her right side. A stranger, elderly, female, with hair in rollers wearing a frilly nightdress, peers at her curiously. Talks to someone outside of Daisy's view.

"He must have done something horrible to her. Men! They're all like that. My old man, he did it. Three times before the police would help. Said it was domestic. Nothing to do with them they said. Horrible it was!"

Now the tinkly voice again.

"Ssh, sssh, Mrs Betts. The new lady is awake now."

No it is not her home. A familiar sinking feeling locates the tinkly voice. It is the type with whom Daisy has had previous dealings. She shuts the right eye again. There is no further need to look. Many starched slim young nurses have had that voice. Now she puts her hand carefully up to her head. Knows before she reaches it that there will be a bandage.

How did she get to this hospital? How long has she been here? The usual questions. Then hard upon them the habitual fear. Who is looking after Deborah?

Memory returns. Her shoulders begin to shake. This time events had occurred in a new setting. Jerry in an unfamiliar position as her passenger. She, the nameless driver at the wheel of Adeline, the car named for his mother.

Daisy's sympathy when the old lady, Adeline Angel, had died had been perfunctory. Jerry's mother, crotchety and critical, had not liked her.

Not the real thing, old Adeline would say sourly.

Sweet Adeline, Jerry had hummed as she drove, using the jazzy new version of the old barber shop quartet, made popular by Jerry Angel on his piccolo.

A ridiculous instrument, Daisy had always thought, but in Jerry's hands, it had changed its status from that of a toy to that of a concert platform instrument. An irritating tune,

Daisy had once mocked, until she was silenced by the speed with which the haunting refrain became top of the pops.

Jerry had hummed and she had sat silently as they drove towards Brighton for him to join the other veteran car drivers in the annual Old Jalopies Race. As soon as there was an audience, Jerry would take the wheel. Since the first Adeline Race Day eight years ago, it had become an annual British event. It was the event at which Jerry, monitored by the media, took out of her covers his treasured Adeline.

One year they had made a film about the old jalopies and used as the theme music Jerry's tune 'Adeline'. Secretly she and Deborah called it 'asinine', but despite their barely concealed contempt the film made money for the Angels just as the piccolo playing did.

"A musician's career can be short. I need all the money we can pull in," Jerry had said. "I need better and better publicity. I need *you*, Daisy; you're a damn good publicist. That University who underpay you as a press officer, they don't value your talents. I need you to work for *me*. To work for us, all of us. We are a family, Daisy. We need to stand together."

What Jerry needed, with his extravagant tastes in women and cars (Daisy who drove the cars, knew about the women) was a fortune, she had thought bitterly.

But the wheedling went on. We are a family. A Jewish family must pull together to stick together. On and on. You're talented Daisy. You're a writer; you're a good publicity writer. You're wasted at that University. They can get some academic wimp to do what they need. They don't need you.

Finally she crumbled, gave up her own writing and her University post and became an underpaid, undervalued publicist for Jerry Angel Productions.

Lying in the hospital bed she can still hear the piping refrain. Louder than she had heard it in the car. Will yourself

back to sleep, she urges. Will yourself to die. She feels too
dead now to care that some parts of her are evidently alive.
It is but an image, whatever reality had been left to her had
died in the vehicle.

Jerry in the passenger seat correcting her every move.
The only times she ever drove him were before races or
charity events. Jerry shouting at her as she drove.

"What does it matter? What does one more woman
matter? You bitch. You exasperating bitch! We shall be late
for the start if you don't bloody drive fast!"

She drove on. Faster. What *did* one more woman matter?
Jerry collected women like he collected cars. Longed for
them. Fantasised over them. Raced them. Treasured them.
Exhausted them. Discarded them.

A large and growing collection of women now and little
genuine affection left between them. He had worn it out.
Yet still he assured her that she was the only woman who
mattered in his life. She was his wife. She was his *Jewish* wife.
More significantly, as Jewish law insists that a child is only
Jewish if born of a Jewish mother (the father's standing being
for once irrelevant) she was now a Jewish mother, so Jerry's
beloved Deborah was entitled to take up the family faith.

As Deborah was alarmingly rebellious and might have
views of her own, Daisy foresaw in the future trouble
between Jerry and his precious daughter.

Already Deborah was not quite as precious as Sweet
Adeline, Daisy had thought bitterly, as she watched the
speedometer and Jerry's temper rise.

Cars seldom rebel although they are prone to mishaps.
Daughters, if not entirely dutiful, find they are less well cared
for. Vintage and veteran cars are, after all, irreplaceable. And
entirely British. Less than dutiful daughters are in this case
half American and could always be replaced.

God may say to Jerry be fruitful and multiply but with the best faith in the world, today's well injected sperm cannot produce a Vintage model constructed between 1919 and 1930, nor can it bring forth a Veteran beauty built between 1905 and 1919.

Daughters on the other hand can be spermed into existence any day of the week. All that is needed is fertile female soil, preferably Jewish.

Jerry had stopped shouting. She slowed down. He mouthed at her ferociously:

"I've told you, you are the only woman that counts. But you must leave me my freedom!"

She could no longer take it. She needed to get the sentences out before the stammering started.

"Sure I'm the only woman that counts. I count alright. One! Two! Three! Four!

Penny! Jenny! Jill! Phyllis! Even Lol, *my friend*, you think I don't know about those two days in Amsterdam? You think I can't count? And that's only *this* year. Oh y-yes, I'm the only w-woman in your life that c-counts."

Some grains of sense inside her whispered: "Foolish, you are being foolish."

Jerry lunged at her. In terror she missed the brake, put her foot on the accelerator. He smashed at her skull as she drove. Sliced her head with his palm. Viciously knocked her face onto the wheel.

"THEY DON'T MATTER…THEY DON'T MATTER…THEY DON'T MATTER…"

Jerry struck at her with every word. She had braked and the car had skidded to a stop. Dragging her by the hair he banged her against the window. There was a splintering of glass.

Damage to his treasured Adeline halted him.

He got out to examine the car, whistling Sweet Adeline under his breath.

The last thought she could remember having before she blacked out was that the Jerry of a decade ago, an affectionate despot, yes, but suave and seemingly sane, had grown unruly with madness. She could take no more of his rule, his rages, his excesses......as she fell unconscious she heard him whistling the tune.

Daisy reopens the eye that works. Questions can be delayed. If she is alive, someone will provide the answers. Only her anxiety about Deborah cannot wait. Will Jerry protect Deborah as he will Adeline in Daisy's absence? How can she trust him any longer to protect anyone, anything, dear to her? She shapes her lips for the correct words:

"May I sit up?"

She knows Tinkle Tones will hear her.

"Of course Mrs Angel. Nice to have you with us. Such a nasty accident. Now would you like to meet the other ladies on your ward?"

She has no wish to meet other ladies. She is not a lady. She has nothing in common with them.

She makes a smiling mouth.

"Yes, that will be nice."

Names. Faces. Curious. Eager. Faces. Names. Eager. Curious. Fade. Blur.

Blur around her.

The nurse is tidying her ladies up. One is causing a spot of bother.

"Come along Greta. It will be good for you to join in things just for once."

She receives no response.

"Now Greta," Tinkle Tones chides, "Wouldn't you like to meet Mrs Angel? She is a New Lady like you."

A cold resolute voice from somewhere down the ward says: "No."

Daisy is mildly amused. She wonders idly to whom the cool voice belongs. Sounds young.

"Greta's new too. A day or two ahead of you though." The nurse lowers her voice confidentially.

"Between you and me, Mrs Angel, she's a bit of a difficult case. Taken an overdose. Oh dear, I shouldn't have let that slip. Student type. You know the sort? Well, of course you do, you once worked at the University didn't you?"

Worked yes. Past tense like everything she had tried to achieve on her own.

"I do not feel you are giving the University your undivided attention any more, my dear Daisy," the Vice Chancellor had said after Jerry had driven and played his way back into her hard-won professional life.

She had held down that post as University Press Officer for three tough years after Jerry had deserted her and Deborah for the first time. Within three months after Jerry's return, he had taken over her office fax machine, the photocopier, her secretary, and the three phone lines. Even the Vice Chancellor's flexibility could not withstand this outrageous assault on academia.

"I am afraid, Daisy, you will have to choose between the University's business and your husband's business."

Her silence had forced him to proceed.

"Let us say then that as a temporary measure you will leave us to sort out ourselves in this department without your invaluable help, whilst you return home to sort out matters there. I am very sorry to lose you, Daisy. You are a first rate press officer."

"How glad you must have been to leave all those student types."

Tinkle Tones is gushing.

"So much more exciting working for your husband. How lucky you are. Fancy your husband getting those amazing sounds out of a tiny piccolo. Such a clever man isn't he? How proud you must be…"

"Proud, oh yes."

The white starched skirts scuttle away. A jumbo television is wheeled through the swing doors. The women sit up, comb their hair, shuffle about. Pink fluffy slipperettes rush to and fro fetching easy chairs. Pillows are plumped. Daisy's good eye wearily follows the bustle.

Obviously it is television time which from her knowledge of hospital routines means teatime also. Another trolley on which reside sturdy white cups and saucers clatters in.

How many wards has she been in now?

"I can count alright. One. Two. Three. Four."

Bruised eyes. Cut lips. Fractured skull. Broken arm. She is too tired to recall other injuries, other wards. And still she stays to write his publicity. Bolster his image. Speak loyally about him to Deborah and Lol's children.

Her eye and head ache intolerably. What does it matter? Sleep is what she needs. She needs to sleep away yesterday's horrors.

Was it yesterday? She realises she has no idea of time or date. Jerry was supposed to collect Deborah and Lol's three children in time to watch the race. Had Debbie seen her with her face massacred?

"We knew you would want to see the programme, Mrs Angel."

Tinkle Tones is back at her bedside.

"The other ladies wouldn't miss it for the world, would we ladies?"

Daisy hears an obedient affirmative chorus.

"Want to see what?" Daisy asks fatigued, fearful.

"The Old Jalopies Race of course. I expect your husband will be interviewed after the race. Perhaps he will even give us that tune."

"He must have done something horrible to her."

The voice of the rollered woman drifts over to her.

"Wasn't the race, um, yesterday? I mean a few days ago…"

"Poor dearie, you've been out for the count. Shame, that's what it is."

Mrs Betts, in the next bed, stares at Daisy with dark inquisitive eyes. Takes in Daisy's expensive silk nightdress.

Does Mrs Betts know? Do they all know?

"Men, they are all like that."

Daisy wants to cry out that Jerry is not like that. Jerry is different. She finds she cannot voice her own lies.

Mrs Betts smiles at her kindly.

"You'll be alright in here. The doctors will pull you round."

Daisy notices the rollers have vanished. Mrs Betts' hair is coiffured in high bangs round her little head. She is putting on dark blusher. Smudges it as she prepares for the small screen.

"The Race was yesterday dearie. But they've got a film, and then some interviews."

"We mustn't tire our new lady, Mrs Betts," the nurse admonishes. Then she lowers her tone again as she turns to Daisy.

"I hope you don't mind my telling them who you were. Quite a thrill for them to be in a ward with a celebrity's wife. I expect your husband will visit you after his TV appearance. Such a nasty accident. He seemed positively shaken."

"No, I don't mind," she hears herself say.

One day she will wake up to find she has turned into an Angel Ansamachine.

What additional information did the nurse impart to her ward? She hopes at least the girl with the cool voice had shown no interest. What was her name? Greta, that was it.

Someone turns on the television. The ladies gather round. Greta turns away, two bare shoulders exposed above the white sheets.

"Greta? Don't you want to watch?"

"No. I am about to wash my hair."

Greta sits up, naked. Thin pale body. Unselfconsciously she slips from the sheets to the side of the bed. Slowly she pulls on white briefs, faded blue jeans. Holding a towel, naked from the waist up, she wanders off in the direction of the bathroom.

The race has started. Daisy prays her face may remain immobile when Jerry appears on the screen.

Suddenly a posse of student doctors follow a stern faced man down the room towards Daisy's bed.

"Oh dear, Mrs Angel, doctor's round, you'll have to miss it."

A brief painful examination. The stern faced doctor pulls curtains around her bed, points out the fracture above her eye. The student medics make notes of the bruises. Something about a retina which she cannot catch. Two deep gashes. The older man dismisses the students.

"The friend who brought you in said it was an accident?"

Shame colours her cheeks.

He smiles at her. "I told her not to worry. You too, Mrs Angel. You reached us just in time. Pretty bad fractures. Displaced retina. But they will heal. I am more worried about the head injuries. We shall give that a few days."

She cries out as he touches her.

"Hum, I thought so. Let us wait and see."

Finally she finds a voice.

"Thank you. I am grateful."

A pause. Resolutely she says: "I am sure you understand?"

"Yes, Mrs Angel, I do. I saw your husband last night. I told him you were lucky to still have your sight. No point in mincing matters."

She is relieved the doctors know.

"I left him a worried man. Indeed I hope I left him a highly anxious man. Quite correct in the circumstances."

Embarrassment floods over her.

"No need for distress," he says gently. "What I say to one person is not necessarily what I choose to say to another. The window shattered and your head and eye were injured. That is all there is to it."

He puts out his hand to shake hers. She notices a wide gold ring.

For a few seconds Daisy wonders whom the doctor is protecting, her or the celebrity?

A spurt of malice infects her. She wants revenge. In her ministry voice: "You shall not take revenge, nor bear any grudge, but you shall love your neighbour as yourself." (Leviticus 19 verse 18.)

The television programme draws to a close. She hears Jerry's laugh. The other professional racing drivers look with respect as he lounges on Adeline's bonnet. Jerry then perches on top of the car, piccolo in hand. The tune starts up, sharp and haunting. The ladies in the ward hum along to Sweet Adeline.

Daisy looks at Jerry's smug fingers. Jerry's white hands around his instrument then his slim fingers stroking Adeline's back. The credits appear and the music fades.

Daisy glances down the ward. Cross legged on the floor

Greta, oblivious to everyone, rubs her thick brown hair with a towel. Her jeans show damp patches. Still naked from the waist up, her small breasts look like under-ripe apples. On the floor beside her are three half-finished jigsaws and an untidy pile of books. Nothing else in Tinkle Tones' territory is out of place.

She watches the young girl pull on an old rust cashmere with a round neck and puffed sleeves, the kind upper class young women once wore with pearls. Greta's jumper has a tear under the sleeve. She wears no jewellery. She would look pretty with a jewel around her throat.

Daisy's hand touches the silver necklace around her own neck. Her neck hurts as she does so. She thought all pain was supposed to be located in her head. She has a ridiculous impulse to offer the young woman her chain.

Greta's rust sweater is tight across the small breasts, tugs up, leaving a gap between her torn top and faded jeans. Immersed in her jigsaw she is unaware of the older woman's attentive gaze. Pale blue pieces of sky litter the floor.

"Nearly time for Visitors," tinkles the nurse. "Tidy up now Greta."

The girl laconically neatens the jigsaw, climbs slowly out of the jeans, pulls the rust cashmere over her tousled hair, folds it over and over until it is a narrow strip of orange wool, flaring above the white sheets. Then, again comfortably naked, she slips between the sheets without disturbing the orange band. The women eye her with disapproval but her disdainful expression inhibits comments.

By visiting hour, Daisy has struggled into the white towel robe which has appeared in her locker along with yesterday's unopened mail for Jerry, two new paperbacks, and six pages of the publicity article she had been engaged upon.

Her forehead, skull and left eye have been rebandaged

but the pain is worse. The bruises on her face have been tinctured and left uncovered.

When Jerry walks into the ward he looks beyond her, hugs her with care, and throws six dozen red roses onto the bed. He has of course forgotten that she is not one of his women who like roses. Carnations would have been her choice. Jerry does not attempt to kiss her right cheek. Perhaps that too is marked. Is she an obvious exhibit of domestic violence? A vulgar display of a private quarrel. Jerry hates vulgar displays.

"Whatever is harmful to you, do not do to your neighbour. This is the essence of the Torah; the rest is commentary."

Hillel (1ˢᵗ century BC) has summarised the whole of the Torah thus, whilst standing on one foot.

Jerry shifts from one foot to the other uneasily.

"I'll just get us some privacy," he says irritably. "I hadn't realised you would still be in a public ward."

She wants to retort: "Oh there's no need for privacy here! We are all the same. A bunch of failed battered wives, suicides, abortions! Typical messy women's ward."

She is however afraid to say anything. She does not yet know what ground they are on.

Jerry glances round at the nurse hovering accessibly.

"Could my wife have screens around her bed, Nurse Williams," he asks graciously. "Would a cup of coffee, no milk, no sugar, be a possibility?"

Tinkle Tones is delighted he knows her name.

"Of course, Mr Angel. We loved your programme. Such a pity your wife had to miss it. Doctor's visit you know. We don't usually give visitors coffee, but just this once…"

She gushes away and screens are brought.

They are alone.

Jerry holds one of her hands. Strokes it carelessly. Daisy

recalls the attentive way he had stroked Adeline only a few minutes ago. Her husband looks stricken. The doctor must have chosen his words well.

"Honey, I'm sorry. I cannot bear to see you like this. I told them it was an accident. Will you forgive me?"

Daisy could have written his script better but could not have performed it so well.

"Forgive you? For telling lies to save your face? Or for injuring mine?"

Her voice is rough edged. Hard. Something stony appears behind Jerry's contrite expression.

"HONEY! That is a trifle provocative isn't it? I have said I am sorry."

He is warning her.

"Please sweetie, try and understand." He softens his own rough edges.

"I don't know what happened. I wouldn't have had it happen for all the world. Sometimes I think I am going crazy with these rages."

Daisy remembers the Tavington Clinic to which Jerry had sent *her* to sort out their troubles. He felt *she* needed help. The counsellor had eventually seen them both. At that interview Jerry had seethed silently and refused to talk. He spoke later to the counsellor on his own.

"You must be careful not to provoke your husband," the counsellor had quietly summed up. "He can get quite difficult, even dangerous when provoked. He is liable to flare up at the slightest criticism. Try to keep him calm dear. I am sure it will be in your own best interest."

"Usually I don't provoke him," Daisy had said stubbornly.

Reluctantly the counsellor had admitted: "There may be an area in Mr Angel's mind, over and above anger due to natural provocation, which could lead to uncontrollable rages. I hesitate to use the word but it could be a slight inclination towards a psychopathic tendency. Nothing to worry about of course, if you do your part, keep things steady."

Jerry was given no instructions to do his part or to keep things steady.

"There is one and the same law for you and the resident stranger in your midst, a law binding on your descendants for all time, you and the alien are alike before the Lord." (Numbers 15, verses 15, 16).

Ben Azzai and Rabbi Akiva (50-135 C.E.) may have thought there was one and the same law for man and for woman, but the Rabbis are wrong.

Keep things steady. Do your part.

"It is OK Jerry. Shall we try and forget it?"

The ice behind his eyes melts.

"Sure, sure. That's my girl! Now see what I have for you."

His leather bag bulges. Preserved fruit. Chocolate creams. Vintage claret. A pack of new pens and more unopened mail.

She grimaces.

"Come on sweetie," he coaxes. "You know I can't deal with that sort of thing. Think of it as therapy."

He kisses an unbruised part of her face. She nods. A tired acquiescence.

"Where's Deb? What have you told her? Who is she with?"

"Don't worry. Deborah is fine. She's with Lol and the kids and eager to see you. Just thinks you've had a tumble in the car."

His voice reassures. He is confident, back on his territory.

"I had to get to the race, had to be there at the start. I knew you would understand. So I picked up the children as we arranged, left you at Lol's and told her to see to things. You'd have wanted me to do that honey wouldn't you? Everything as normal, eh? I just didn't know how bad you were, not till the doc said all those dreadful things."

Will Jerry ask for forgiveness of his sins against her on Yom Kippur, Daisy wonders idly. Probably not. He has never managed to accept the concept of sin in relation to his own behaviour. If he did ask for Divine grace, she doubted it would be granted, for the Talmud states that verbal atonement is insufficient. Grace requires genuine repentance, great determination to desist from repetition and a positive attempt to make amends.

Preserved fruit, chocolate creams and the wrong floral tribute will not count as making amends.

Suddenly she is aware with frightening clarity that he will never desist from repetition; there will be only more of the same and worse. She will have to decide, on her own, having no friend or confidante free of Jerry's thrall, whether to stay for more of the same or not.

Jerry is gathering new lines.

"Sweetie, I'd never had dumped you if I'd realised what a state you were in. I just didn't figure it out. What with the race and the cars. But Lol's been fantastic. I'll go there on Friday for Kiddush and see the Shabat in with her and the family. Then Lol will bring Deborah in to see you. You'll be more healed up by then."

Jerry is impatient with their tête-à-tête. He jerks the screens apart and looks through the gap.

"Who IS that? That pretty young girl in the end bed?"

Jerry's eyes are on Greta's bare shoulders, the tops of her breasts showing above the sheets.

Her half completed jigsaw is on the floor. She sits staring into space.

"Her name is Greta. From the University. Took an overdose, seems frails and sick. She's very quiet, a nice relief after the other women. I half thought of saying hello…"

"Great idea baby! Be good for her to have you to talk to. How about I go and give her the new hardback I bought you, I can always get you another copy?"

Without waiting for an answer, Jerry swoops, book in hand, to the end of the ward. He sits on Greta's bed attempting to magnetise her. Greta glances in Daisy's direction with an ironic look.

Jerry returns bubbling over.

"You'll find her an unusual girl. Interesting. Not that she said much but she had that certain look. Needs cheering up. Like you do. I told her to keep the book, OK about that? Anything else you need? Just say the word baby! You know you are the only woman who counts for me. Got a couple of important calls to make so shall have to tear myself away. Don't forget to listen to my broadcast tonight. I'll get the nurse to get you headphones."

Daisy wonders how you can attach headphones without further damage to the head?

He kisses her quickly, pushes back the screens and rushes down the ward. Jerry Angel is leaving. There is no more need for privacy. At Greta's bed he pauses, says something. The girl stares straight ahead without answering.

For several days Daisy lies quietly then the doctor says she may try moving around. Jerry visits more frequently than in previous hospitals. The ladies on the ward love it. Greta remains impervious to his attentions. He brings Deborah. He brings mail. Bills. A white filing tray for efficiency. A pocket word processor for Daisy. Books for Greta. Discovers Greta reads Rilke. Buys her a copy in hardback. It lies unopened on her locker. A monster box of hard centres for

the staff. Soft centres for the patients. Peppermint creams
for Daisy. Champagne and brandy liqueur chocolates for
Greta. Remembers carnations for his wife. Gives Greta the
red roses. Then a single orchid.

"That poor kid," he says appealingly. "No-one ever visits
her. It is the least you and I can do. Give her the odd
present, cheer her up…"

Daisy herself talks reticently to Greta and discovers the
girl dislikes company, does not easily engage in conversations
and is uninterested in material possessions.

Jerry's orchid remains on Greta's bed for several hours
and would have died there, as indeed the roses had done, had
not Nurse Williams put it in the ward's finest vase.

"Not everyone is brought bouquets by famous musicians,"
she informs Greta.

"It is not a bouquet, merely a stiff displeasing single
bloom," Greta reports pedantically. "Flowers should be left
where they belong, in gardens and fields."

Daisy grins.

Occasionally she and Greta swap books or anecdotes
about Brighouse University where each believe they have
failed. Daisy for allowing Jerry to take over her office and
procure her dismissal, Greta for having failed to obtain a
degree.

"I did not complete an insignificant course. Breakdowns.
That is what they called them. As if one is a car. One is not
a car. That is a line that strange man who visits you with
alarming parcels would not understand. That man runs or
sell cars or musical instruments does he not?"

Daisy smiles with pleasure. It is the most engaging
description of Jerry's profession that she has heard.

"That strange man is a musician who collects classic cars,
also my husband."

"Poor you!" Greta says matter-of-factly before returning slowly to her own story.

"Those at the University were ignorant people. Breakdowns was not what I was about at all. There was not anything inside me to breakdown. I was being something else at the time."

Daisy tries to understand. To help the conversation along as she does at Jerry's dinner parties.

"What did you DO at College? Did the breakdowns interfere with your exam? Is that why you got sad and sick?"

Instantly she recognises she has struck the wrong note. Greta's face freezes. She withdraws into herself.

"DO Mrs Jerry Angel. What did I DO? I try never to do anything. Why do you always ask about doing? Never do you inquire about being. You are after all just like the rest. Goals and achievement, they are the treasures you store up for yourselves. You have no conception of beingness. Only a concept of wealth and activity."

"Do not store up for yourselves treasure on earth, where it grows rusty and moth eaten, and thieves break in to steal it. Store up treasures in heaven, where there is no moth and no rust to spoil it, no thieves to break in and steal. For where your wealth is, there will your heart be also." (Matthew 6, verse 19).

Daisy realises with surprise that in Greta's Christian presence, she herself has switched to the Gospel. Momentarily she feels guilty. Greta however is right. There is wealth in being which the doers like Jerry never have time for.

Greta for her part is angry, will not talk to Daisy for four days, lies in bed stony and unrelenting.

Jerry has been to Amsterdam again, to arrange a new musical show and to attend a classic car meeting. He returns to the hospital, showering the ladies with fresh red tulips from Amsterdam.

Jerry has discovered Greta's passion for jigsaws. Brings her an elaborately drawn view of London, five thousand pieces. She glances at the picture.

"I have had that little one. It will be hard to find one that I haven't done or that I am interested in doing."

Laconically she hands it back to him. Unopened.

"That kid is pretty hard to please," Jerry reports to his wife, but she notes, without his habitual irritation.

With a familiar ache, Daisy recognises that Greta's constant rebuffs are challenging Jerry to ever greater inventiveness.

After he leaves, Greta walks quietly over to Daisy's bed to continue their conversation as if there had been no four day break.

"For my diligence and intellectual aptitude, the University authorities awarded me a Sick Degree with a fancy Latin name. Does that satisfy your achievement oriented soul? Also failure to achieve a Well Degree is not what drew me towards death. I embrace death. I have always embraced death. I do not talk about it. I do not believe in talk and babble. Your car man babbles."

"Do not go babbling on like the heathen who imagine that the more they say the more likely they are to be heard." (Matthew 6 verse 7).

By Jerry's faith, it is Greta who is a heathen. But it is a Jewish Angel trait to babble, to wish to be heard above all men.

"I do not expect you to understand about death," Greta says firmly.

"I should like to understand," Daisy says.

Her bruises are mending but there is a complication in the repair to the eye. A new consultant is called in. Daisy must again rest. She is to spend another week at least in hospital. Deborah is missing her. Jerry is becoming impatient about the amount of work piling up that Daisy cannot do in hospital.

Then the doctor tells Daisy that the publicity writing done on the tiny word processor is straining her eyes. Jerry concedes but asks if she can occasionally draw. Given permission, he brings in her drawing board and pencils and asks her to start some publicity drawings of the cars. Daisy convinces the doctors it is good for her to be occupied.

The conflicting demands made upon her are too much for her to deal with. Wife. Mother. Business partner. Not her business. Nothing to do with her. Business partner. Wife. Mother. But who is to mother her?

Round and round goes her brain. She realises she wants very little except some peace and a chance to talk further to the curious self-contained girl in the end bed. Could she be making her first friend?

Patiently Daisy tries to draw out Greta. It is not the young woman's first suicide attempt. There have been three or four. Daisy wonders what the problem is.

"It is not a problem," Greta says coldly. "Except to those like you. I have no wish to get up in the mornings. There is nothing for me to do because I do not believe in doing anything. There is nothing for me to get up for. I am content lying here, alone. People talk about getting up as though it had something to offer. I do not see life that way. I see the kind of life your car man engages in as entirely negative. For me death is positive."

She is detached but firm.

"I do not understand why these doctors interfere with my desire for death. It is nothing to do with them. Doctors, they are all the same."

"The heart of the wise is in the house of mourning but the heart of fools is in the house of mirth." (Ecclesiastes 7 verse 4).

Daisy has lived alone in the crowded House of Mirth for more than a decade. There may be more comfort in the House of Mourning.

This strange girl with her strange enduring sickness sees suicide as an everyday occurrence. Part of her plan. Except that plan is not one of Greta's words. Suicide is no more untoward than domestic violence. Daisy finds it easy to tell her about the incident in the car. The incidents before this one. Ten years of incidents. She feels no disloyalty. Greta neither comments nor judges, merely pays attention.

Greta's persistent preoccupation with death becomes Daisy's private obsession. The girl in the end bed has no wish to awake in the mornings, but for the older woman, her first waking thought is now about Greta.

The young girl tells her lightly that no-one has cared for her. It is not something she minds.

"Why should people care for one another? It is not necessary. We all die. We all die alone. It is better to live remembering that."

Greta, who has no interest in the magnetic Jerry Angel, who is disdainful of Jerry's efforts to please her, is a fresh experience. Slowly she begins to talk more about herself. She has been adopted and despises her adopted parents.

"They are not real. They try too hard. Like religious converts," she says scathingly.

To Daisy these people sound kindly, reasonable parents. To Greta they are intruders. Overtakers and caretakers in what should have been her own life.

"The man who called himself Father is thankfully dead. Before he died he repelled me by his coarse food habits and his plastic raincoat."

"And your 'mother'?"

"She is *not* my mother. She works for the Red Cross

and bakes me homemade biscuits. She believes she is well bred but she calls napkins 'serviettes'. A vulgar woman who keeps asking me to come 'home' and visit her. I have no home so there is nowhere to visit. Once I looked for my real mother, but the search led nowhere. I decided it was pointless, she would be nothing to me in any case."

Daisy wonders how the young woman feels about her failed search for her mother, just as she had earlier speculated about her failed attempt to obtain a degree. Now she knows better than to voice such thoughts aloud.

Privacy is Greta's most critical possession. She trusts no-one, allows nobody near her. Passively accepts people's attention as she does the hospital food.

Jerry visits both women daily, bombards Greta with entertainment and Daisy with work. He filters white wine into a thermos for Greta, brings Daisy fresh ground coffee so that she may stay alert. He has taken several new sets of publicity photos of Adeline and he tells Daisy he needs twenty-four intricate drawings of the car to accompany them. These will be blown up and multiplied from a dozen different angles. It is for some new campaign he is mounting.

Daisy pays very little attention.

The photos and drawings are to be printed in garish orange, startling red and shining white rather than in the actual car colours. Then they will be mounted on a six foot board.

Daisy tries hard to concentrate.

"But all the cars will look alike. It will be incredibly complex to sort them out," she says. "I don't understand why you want me to draw them this way."

Being less interested than usual in Jerry's projects she does not press the point.

"You do the work, sweetie, then I am going to have something so clever done with them, it will just be the biggest surprise you have ever had," he says enthusiastically.

The drawings are so complex that Daisy, bent over her drawing board most waking hours, finds the strain on her one good eye intolerable. One afternoon she bursts into tears from pain and weariness.

"Why on earth do you slave like that for the man who put you in here?" Greta asks. "Why do you stay with him at all?"

Daisy is no longer sure.

From the outside she is back doing the same work for him. Apparently adhering to the same values. Accepting the same insults. Living the same lies…

But inside something is changing. She no longer believes she is an integral part of the Angel Empire. Certainly not its core. She may never walk out, she is after all a Jewish wife, but Adeline and Jerry are now pinned to her drawing board rather than fastened inside her head.

Out of habit she still repairs some of the broken pieces. Yes, out of habit. Duty. Dying affection. There is also Deborah. She has become a Jewish mother.

She is marking time, gathering strength, while drawing Adeline.

There is no way she can explain this to the young woman in her twenties.

"Once Jerry loved me, once he tried to understand me. Once, and not for long. Then we got married. I began to help him. I had Deborah. He had Adeline. I have gone on helping him. It is part of what is left of the love I once felt. I am still trying to help him because I don't know how to help myself."

"Oh LOVE!" Greta says scornfully. "It isn't him who needs help!"

The subject is dropped. Daisy spends painful hours drawing and redrawing minute portions of Adeline's body, occasionally Greta reads poetry aloud to her.

When the sketches are finished Jerry carries them off in triumph. That day the doctors say Daisy may return home in a few days. Despite the fact that her damaged body has after all mended reasonably well, she is curiously depressed.

Visiting hours, once seen as the high point of a routine day, now seem an exasperating interruption in her slow negotiations with Greta. After a series of icy rebuffs, she has ceased her well-intentioned but clumsy overtures. Instead of trying to draw the girl out, she has been trying to draw her. Pin her elusive spirit to a sheet of A4 cartridge paper. Her sketches fail to catch the flickering emotions behind Greta's frozen eyes.

"Always you must *do* something. If you are not doing something for that car man of yours, you now find even in me, a thing to do."

Greta's voice this time however is not quite as hard as it has been.

"Nearly time for Visitors. Back in your beds, Ladies. Greta put your top on, there will be Gentlemen here. Come along you two chatty ones, clear up your little messes."

Nurse Williams admonishes the two grown women as if they had been children.

"Well, Mrs Angel, your generous husband has told me he will be bringing something special into the ward today."

Jerry attempts to walk majestically into the ward but is hampered by two unwieldy gigantic parcels, one over six feet long. A porter is helping him.

"Dear Nurse Williams, what I really need is a television trolley," he says puffing. "Ah, thank you so much."

Aplomb restored, Jerry wheels in a huge clinking crate

on top of which is balanced a six foot long, three foot wide, wooden box tied with orange, red and white ribbons and bows. He deposits the crate at the foot of Daisy's bed, then wheels the great wooden object over to Greta.

Daisy cuts the cord and is stunned to discover it contains one dozen magnums of champagne.

She rushes down the ward to Greta where Jerry perches on Greta's bed, carelessly stroking the girl's hair, trying to get her attention. The girl lies on her stomach with her eyes closed.

"Come on Greta baby, do open it."

"Come on Greta," Daisy says enthusiastically. "Do open it. Mine is champagne. Bottles and bottles. I cannot imagine what yours is."

Jerry glances at his wife approvingly before turning back to the young woman. His hand rests on her hair then moves down. Daisy watches him stroke Greta's bare neck and shoulders.

"Greta baby, you'll never have seen one like this. You won't have had one like this. You'll be spending a lot of time working out this one baby! I had it made especially for you."

In extreme exasperation, Greta pulls away from him and sits up testily.

"GO AWAY!" she says tensely. "I am trying to sleep. Daisy, take this odious man away. If YOU want to see what is in this ridiculous box then open it, but GO AWAY!"

"Yes, sweetie, you open it for Greta," Jerry says as if he has not noticed the girl's annoyance.

"OK I shall open it," Daisy soothes.

She is no longer sure to whom she is addressing herself. Jerry's hand on the young woman's body gives her the same distress she feels when he strokes Adeline. But Greta's disinterest upsets her also. Obviously Jerry has gone to great lengths to please her. She knows she, too, is desperate to please Greta. She is aware she has spent a decade pleasing Jerry. She feels she is on the edge of tears.

Why on earth has Jerry brought her a crate of champagne? What precious object can be in this parcel for Greta? Why must she leave this safe and happy place tomorrow?

Carefully she cuts the masses of orange, red and white bows and ribbons. There are layers of tissue paper in alabaster, crimson and copper. Her hands unpack the frost white folds over an apricot sunset. She lets the ruby ribbons, snow white and ochre bows fall and loop in fire glow rings onto the brown wooden ward floor.

Inside the box is an enormous wooden board. On it is a mass of fiery orange, red and white dazzling designs and pieces and shapes and segments, all fractured by tiny black lines. The colours jumble. The fire dances. The tangerine flames lick and twist. The wooden pieces part and move, edged by the fractured black lines.

It is the largest brightest wooden jigsaw she has ever seen.

What is the picture? There is no picture. Well, there is no *one* picture. Or is there?

Slowly the colours collapse, the shapes soften, settle. Orange. Red. White. Orange. Red. White. Familiar. Frighteningly familiar.

Her drawings. These are her twenty-four intricate drawings, drawn in pain from duty, twenty-four drawings of Adeline. Imposed. Superimposed. Sorted. Distorted. Copied. Recopied. The whole jigsaw is made up of a dozen different views of Jerry's priceless lady; upside down, back to front, lengthways, sideways…wherever she looks, Daisy sees red, orange, white flashing shining shapes of Adeline.

Sweet Adeline six foot long. Sweet Adeline three foot wide. Every line is a line she has drawn herself. Jerry's treasured lady turned into a toy for Greta.

"There are ten thousand pieces!" Jerry announces proudly. "It's the largest jigsaw the Western world has ever seen! I have had it made especially for you, Greta. Handmade for you baby! It is for you, Greta."

He leans over to stroke her hair again. Lets his long slim manicured hand rest carelessly on her prone body.

"And half of that champagne is for you, Greta. Well maybe more than half. Daisy is coming home. There's plenty of booze at home. I am sure Nurse Williams will let you girls have a splendid party tonight to celebrate Daisy's last evening."

Ten thousand pieces of Adeline. *Her work.* The hours and hours she has spent drawing that car, with her head throbbing, her bad eye tearing at her. A million hours. A million Venus 6B lines. A million pieces of her soul for him to cup up and offer to Greta. To give Adeline, his Adeline, to her friend Greta.

No, not her friend. Nothing has ever been hers.

Daisy walks slowly over to the crate by her bed. Takes two of the champagne bottles and walks back to Greta's bed, swinging them, one in either hand, slowly up and down.

Jerry and Greta watch her mesmerised.

"You BASTARD!" Daisy breathes. Then she starts to scream.

"YOU BASTARD! MY WORK! THAT WAS MY WORK! My work for you like everything of mine has always been for you. You have taken my work over *again*! You have taken my life over. And now you want to take over my first possible friend! You bastard!"

Daisy lets go of one hand, cracks the champagne bottle on to the iron bedstead. The glass splinters. The liquid spurts and bubbles everywhere. All over Jerry's smart navy blue suit. All over Greta's bare shoulders. Champagne trickles down between the girl's apple breasts.

For the first time in her stay at the Brighouse General, Greta laughs. Laughs helplessly. Cannot stop laughing. The other ladies are frozen with amazement.

Daisy raises the second bottle of champagne and brings it down in the direction of Jerry's head. He ducks and the bottle cracks open on the floor. Daisy strides purposefully through the foaming liquid, walks over to the crate and takes two more bottles. She starts towards Jerry swinging them slowly, one bottle in each hand. Jerry begins a hasty retreat in the nurses' direction.

"You had better go!" Daisy says, advancing towards him. She no longer screams. "You had better go now because I am going to break this next bottle over your head. Then the next. Then the next."

In his haste, Jerry collides backwards with Tinkle Tones who scurries forward like an anxious rabbit.

"Nurse Williams, I, er, I, er I think my dear wife is having a little turn…I think, er, it will be, um, best if I pop along now and leave you to deal, with it, I mean her. I mean, well, will you tell her I shall be back later when she has calmed down."

Nurse Williams smiles nervously round her ward. Most of her ladies are transfixed into upright stone statues, perched on edges of beds, gazing at Daisy. Mrs Betts had stopped rollering her hair midway in order to concentrate more fully on events. Tinkle Tones walks up to Daisy and says weakly: "There, there, Mrs Angel," as she tries to disengage one of the bottles from Daisy's grasp.

Daisy is too strong for her, pushes the nurse away.

"SHUT UP NURSE WILLIAMS!" she says. "Just leave me alone."

Still swinging two champagne bottles, she turns and walks over to Greta. There are tears streaming down her cheeks.

"Stop laughing Greta! For God's sake, stop laughing."

"I am not laughing at *you*," Greta says seriously. "I am laughing at the very idea that your car man would imagine I wanted to waste my time putting together ten thousand pieces of his broken down car."

Daisy wants to hug her, but still unsure, says carefully:

"Do you not want this very large jigsaw my husband has made for you?"

"No, I do not want it. As you are the great doer, Daisy, why do you not do something useful with it?"

Greta points to the slightly open window at one end of the ward. Their room is on the sixth floor. Daisy walks over and looks out. There are dozens of male medical students walking about on the grassy area far beneath.

Slowly she pushes the window wide open. Then she returns to Greta's bed. She places the mammoth jigsaw onto the television trolley. Neither of the two women speaks. Greta, naked except for her white briefs, climbs out of her bed. Together they push the trolley containing the oversized luminous Adeline towards the window. Daisy stands silently at the window's edge.

Greta hands her piece after piece, handful after handful, of Adeline's anatomy. One after another, one dozen, two dozen, one hundred, one thousand, two thousand, five thousand, seven thousand, nine thousand, ten thousand wooden pieces scatter and float, orange and red and white, sunshine and fire and light, down through the sunny afternoon on to the necks and shoulders and faces of the surprised young men in the courtyard below.

★ ★ ★ ★

"This is my beloved and this is my friend, oh daughters of Jerusalem…

"Come my beloved, let us go forth into the field…

"Set me as a seal upon thine heart, as a seal upon thine arm, for love is as strong as death."

"The Song of Solomon" 5 verse 16, 7 verse 11, 8 verse 6

REMEMBRANCE SUNDAY

She would rather have taken her photograph.

Several photographs. A ten by eight portrait. A series of portraits. Some in repose. A few shivering on the brink of movement. Catching the steady clear gaze of Beatrice's eyes. Far too clear. Daisy's own vision unsteady as she remembered the penetrating blue of the eyes. Was it the same shade as the shirt? Cornflower blue and white convict stripes. Neat evenly spaced stripes. Nothing flamboyant about Beatrice Lane's appearance. The top button curving gently over two small breasts. Daisy did not feel gentle remembering. She had no great wish to remember. She would rather take photographs.

Black and white of course would not do. Blue comes out black. It was all coming out black. Memory, she realized with frustration, pays little attention to our wishes. Remembrance is defiantly colour blind.

Daisy was waiting for Ben and, with a certain amount of anger, was remembering Beatrice. Memory seemed to be the one feature in her disciplined lifestyle she could not control. Ben she found easier to control, perhaps because, at twenty-eight, the young bookshop owner was the same age as Daisy's tempestuous daughter Deborah and Beatrice's daughter Charlie, the one with her mother's keen blue eyes and stubborn character.

Daisy had exactly an hour before Ben Quirk closed up Quirks the family bookshop, drove to the country and attempted to disturb her. There was no time for memories, no time for feelings that, after all these months, she still could not handle.

In her white walled room she dressed predictably from head to foot in white ... even her red brown plait braided with white ribbon ... Daisy pitted her considerable will against a series of memories which perched like malignant crows on the rims of the chalky leather armchairs. Today's newly purchased seats, like yesterday's hard purchased self, had been taken over by evocations of Beatrice Lane. The woman, it seemed, still possessed an unsurpassed quality for ownership and control.

Daisy, annoyed, pulled at her plait. Neither she nor her new house would brook repossession. She had changed the lenses. She had refocused her attention on her work. And at weekends on Ben. Young Ben was what the quiet bookseller was usually called, as distinct from Old Ben, the famous father, head of the family business, who had made his name and increased his capital as best-selling crime writer Benjamin B Quirk.

Young Ben had been good to Daisy these last hard months, easing her inflexible work routine, encouraging her to have some fun. Daisy doubted if she could have got through the difficult days without Ben's constancy. Momentarily she felt hemmed in by the recognition and tugged again at her hair. Some straggling chestnut brown strands had escaped from the severity of the braid. More brown than chestnut these days but at least the grey was well covered. Her hair

was the one item in her territory Daisy did not want to see
white. At fifty-six she was as vain as Beatrice had accused
her of being at thirty-six during their first heated encounter,
in Beatrice's blazing brown and orange sitting room. An
occasion of furious argument, every syllable of which Daisy
had meticulously recorded on tape.

For a second her eyes flickered indulgently to the Tand-
berg Audio Tutor 771. The faded black print on the front of
the tape recorder stated: "Educational with Dynamic Sound."
Yes, it had certainly been that. She grinned. Automatically
her mind switched down the play button. Suddenly Daisy's
clinical white workplace, whose only consistent noise was
the cold clatter of metallic machinery, was filled with red
hot sounds from the past.

Anger. Arguments. Jokes and joy. A wild hilarity, and
sometimes weariness as the children squabbled. Teatime
tantrums. The constant whirr of the tapes. Always the same
sounds. Then by ten pm ... Deborah and Charlie upstairs
with their homework, the older Beth quietly reading, Nicola
at last in bed ... passion and peace. Uncertain certitudes,
scheduled to last for centuries.

But they had not.

Perhaps colour prints were the answer. Beatrice in some
moods was too vivid, too unpredictable for black and white,
although they grappled with her strength well enough.
Colour photographs would be more appropriate to catch
Beatrice Lane's ash blonde hair, streaked with bands of
grey; yes, colour would do credit to the blue and white
striped convict shirt, and to the soft blue velvet jacket.
The tailored severe surface that hid the tensions within.
Nothing could do credit to the softness of that jacket. How
many months had it been, after their first meeting, before
Daisy had touched the azure blue of that jacket pulled up

high across the shirt, open just slightly at the neck?

Daisy looked out of the window. No houses opposite. Crumpled green woodland for miles. Scratchy brown bark, a few leaves falling onto the window pane. Chosen for the endless unpeopled space. Privacy at last. Green ... everywhere was green. Calm and dull like the walls of the hospital ward she had spent many weeks in after the news. Not that the news had had anything to do with her accident. She had always driven the white sports car too fast. Had always been prone to accidents. Now she lived safely, had sold the car, cycled a lot, lived in the country, surrounded by plenty of solid safe green. She took occasional visits to the sea with Ben, being careful never to visit Cornwall, where every view remorselessly reminded her of the times with Beatrice and the children.

She remembered how Nicola, the youngest, had bubbled with excitement over the pleasures of the small fishing village. Some evenings it had strained their patience trying to persuade the child to get off to bed.

"What's the point?" Nic had said to Beatrice. "Nothing special ever happens after I go. You two only do dull things."

Nothing special, thought Daisy. Just being together by the sea. Today she was glad she did not look out on the sea. The sea was the wrong colour. That was the problem with the sea. Blue like the eyes, like the shirt, like the jacket that buttoned her mind back to the past. Why had Beatrice never taken off that damn jacket? Eighty-two degrees outside the conference room, their first meeting place, all the other women stripping off, and Beatrice Lane, who had carefully described herself as a staid librarian, calmly buttoned up her striped shirt, and hugged the hot velvet jacket more closely about her shoulders.

Daisy looked down at her hands. Short working fingers which not even memory had removed from the typewriter keys. She gave a wry smile. She was after all only an amateur photographer. By trade, if that is what it was, Daisy was a professional writer. Not, she thought grimly, quite as professional as Old Ben Quirk, whose successful pile of glossy hardbacks were lavishly displayed near the Quirks' cash till. A winning situation. At the side of the shop Ben had carefully mounted Daisy's small select number of paperbacks. No, she was certainly no amateur. Amateurs play around with the people's faces. Bits of scenery. Enlarge and diminish landscapes. Move the trees, or the truth, about a bit. Furniture amongst a green wilderness. Professionals do something similar, but they don't play around.

I broke you, she thought pedantically, passion put aside as she carefully typed the words: I BROKE YOU. I stopped you smiling. I stopped that terrifying calm. For a moment, you stopped looking serene and beautiful. What we had was savage. In the mornings we faced the neighbours like middle-aged good companions, hoping they hadn't identified last night's noises, and talked about the children's progress at the village comprehensive. Then at night we touched and tore at each other's flesh and brought each other to the point where peeing and crying was the only relief from so much held in passion. I do not know how to record that with a camera. Difficult being an amateur. Limited skills.

In the early days of the decade with Beatrice, Daisy's skills had been used for research. Questioning, recording, capturing in sound, pinning down words, in tiny fragments of truth which could be collected, collated, refurbished and framed. "Careful you don't set us in amber," Beatrice had warned one day, giving her a hug. Easy to see why Daisy had later turned to photography.

She had recorded everything. The lines and the lies. The struggle to survive. The problems with the children.

The hostility of their fathers. The fears of the custody cases. The faithfulness of their friends. The laughs, most of all the laughs. But never the passion, never the power. Never the Sundays when the children were usually away with their fathers or grandparents.

Daisy glanced down at her wristwatch. Silver, significant and expensive, on a cheap white leather strap. Ben had given it to her for her last birthday. Originally it had possessed a matching silver wristband. Daisy had changed it. There were days when she felt irrationally controlled by Ben's warmth and generosity. Occasionally she made impetuous silly stands, hurting Ben, then deeply regretting it. She still wanted to punish him for things that were not his fault. Just like Old Ben had.

Beatrice had sent her a simple birthday card with a photo of the sea. Inside, she had written 'Love Bea' and the date. Nothing else. For nine and a half years they had continued to send each other cards for birthdays and at Christmas, and from any exotic holidays which they had taken separately. It was called keeping in touch. The last postcard from Beatrice had come a few weeks after the birthday card. Six months ago. It was from Thailand. Then silence. There had been no further postcards. No more could be expected. Communication had closed down. In another month Daisy knew she would face the first Christmas without a card.

The watch, which recorded days as well as time, informed her it was six o'clock Saturday evening. Ben was due to arrive from the bookshop in a little over an hour for what was left of the weekend. Daisy still had a batch of photos to process, another chapter to finish. For a few minutes she felt under siege, then she thought about Ben and relaxed. If she was still writing she could trust Ben to understand. Considerate and caring about her work, he was an excellent

cook who had developed expert nurturing skills from years
of practice in the Quirk household where everyone paid
constant attention to Old Ben's autocratic whims. This year
at least Ben took quiet care of the Sundays.

In view of the lateness of the hour, it would be foolish
to remember those other Sundays. Ben more than anyone
deserved her full attention for at least one day a week. Daisy
could not afford to waste any more time. She flicked open
her work, then shut it again. She put a clean sheet of paper
into the typewriter, took it out, tore it up. You can't tear up
memories. Foolish or not, Daisy could not forget that last
Sunday, despite the fact that it was ten years ago. No, no quite.
It was nine years, eleven months, three weeks, and six days ago.

That particular Sunday morning was with her now.

Beatrice was huddled in their low brown bed. Sobbing
and struggling with the truth she despaired facing and the
risks she feared taking against the cosy life she had built
up, and the pretences she leant on to give her stability in a
profession that offered her little if the reality of her life with
Daisy was exposed. Beatrice's shoulders shuddered. Her eyes.
Daisy had not wanted to look into her eyes. Such wilderness
should be private. Daisy distanced from the distress, had lain
still on the bed, waiting for the storm to subside, waiting for
Beatrice to talk. She felt chilled, already prepared.

"There were so many times I wished you'd go away. Or
wished the book would go away. Even though I needed
you here, wanted you here. But you never did," Beatrice
said still sobbing.

Daisy remembered saying "No I never did." That was all
she could remember saying, though she suspected she had
said a lot more at the time.

"I've lived with what you have been doing, what we
have been doing for years. I've lived with the tapes, with

the words, I've believed in it like you have. I still do. I was almost sorry when the white light got switched off and I was no longer part of the process. When you shut yourself away, spent all your time working, when all we had was the structure, us as a household, the children, it was as if you had stopped paying me any real attention."

Beatrice was crying again. Quite out of control with crying. She would remember that later. She would despise that later. Daisy had denied some of it but she had felt helpless, alienated, not wanting to understand. She had got out of the bed, gone to the bathroom, and brought back two blue loo rolls. "Try these love, maybe you can get through both of them." They had laughed, and held each other. Daisy had thought of the platitudes. We'll win through. We'll try again. We love each other. She had tried them all out in her head. Rejected them all. Had said nothing. She already knew what decisions Beatrice had come to.

Slowly Beatrice spoke again, her words now muffled by the pillow. "Our life has been filled with words, and sounds, but there are words we can't seem to say. We probably shan't be able to say them for a long time." Then she stopped crying and still hanging on to Daisy she said: "You know that I've met somebody else. I know what you think, you think it's absurd. It may turn out to be unimportant, not in the long run, but at this moment it is important for me to go ahead. I have to do that."

Did Daisy say unfairly: "You'll do what you want. You always do what you want." believing it fair at the time? Or did she merely think it? Hurting someone you care about is always fair if you feel hurt yourself. What she did remember saying, apparently unruffled, surprised at how restrained she sounded: "You'll go away for a bit?"

"Oh yes, I'll probably go away for a bit," Beatrice had answered, calm in her turn. "It's what people do, isn't it?" They had both laughed, as if the very suggestion was idiotic, belonged to two other people.

I didn't really want to drive you out, one of them had murmured. Or perhaps they had not. Perhaps that was something one of them had said later. If they had said it at all. "I do love you, you know that." Certainly one of them had said that, or maybe both, said it again and again, like a mantra, an incantation, a protective blanket of words against the horrors to come. Love anyway had in the end very little to do with it. They had gone on loving each other but each small action they took from that Sunday onwards altered the course of the rest of their lives, as those kind of minor alterations do.

Daisy, skilled at recalling acceptable versions, juggled in her mind several accounts of the words they had spoken, then decided she did not remember exactly what had been said. Ten years had given her time enough to rewrite them all. What did remain clear, as clear and as striking as the events of the previous Sunday spent with Ben on a local beach, was not the words at all.

She remembered Beatrice's lips brushing hers, she remembered watching Beatrice's face lift, her lips coming full down covering her own. She took them gently down to Daisy's breast. Daisy's nipples were ready for her mouth. Daisy exuded the emotion and heat she had been stifling in her chilled body for days, as she and Beatrice had prepared for a cold hard Sunday. Beatrice became more passionate than Daisy could ever recall her being. Ironic in the circumstances. While they made love, or perhaps it was just before they were fully folded, Beatrice had whispered: "I'm scared Daisy." It must have been before; they had never had those kind of conversations during.

Strange, Daisy thought, how with men, fucking with men, she had always needed to talk before, after and particularly during. Their bodies were never enough. She had always needed their words to help her connect. Usually their words were not the right ones, and she wished she had written the script herself. To her surprise she did not talk much with Ben at any point. Words were inessential; it was his presence which composed her. Now he would be marking up books, being helpful to customers, getting ready for the long drive. For the next hour there was no bulwark against the imminent haunting.

Daisy's hands roved across Beatrice's thighs. She had pulled the duvet back. It was a November morning, but still warm, and she wanted to see Beatrice's hairs. She was always intrigued by their darkness. Everything else about her was fair.

"Did you know the hairs on the cunt never go grey?" Beatrice had said sleepily. Her cunt was very large compared with the rest of her body. Her shoulders were slim, her tummy flat, her breasts small. Daisy would tease her about them. "Two little white boobs."

Beatrice, grumpy, would retort: "They work all right. Look at the kids."

Yet she had been self-conscious about their size and Daisy had never understood why. Beatrice's small white breasts made her hold her breath as she thought about sucking them. Her small white breasts and her darker cunt. She wanted to trail her fingers through its darkness. Wanted to push hard into its deepness. Push until it hurt. To feel it wet. Feel it hard and wet first before it moved and melted on her pushing finger. It was the second before her hand touched Beatrice. That second was the one she always feared, was always trembling for. It was the guide to her mind, to their minds. Would she part for her finger?

"My palm runneth over," Beatrice once said with delight when she came upon Daisy fast. "I love you dripping all down my hand." Daisy's own hand hurried. Then she stayed it a moment. "Rest a minute," Beatrice had said. Daisy paused. They had time now. How much time did they have? They had all the time in the world because limits had suddenly been set on it.

"Why are you scared?" Daisy had asked. "No need to be." She was scared herself, scared but excited. Beatrice was murmuring: "You are scary, you won't let me retreat." "No I won't." Daisy was relieved that Beatrice knew. Terrible things were to overtake them and she felt secure lying there beside Beatrice. Even safe. She did not usually have time to work out what she felt. Not when they were loving. There wasn't usually time for dissection. Bodies fly too fast. Minds tip over bodies' edges. That Sunday was more gradual. They were both planning it out delicately. They both wanted it to be right. They both wanted to let go yet keep in each other's hold. Be able to recall some of it later. That loving was crucial Daisy had thought at the time and certainly later.

She had come first willingly, slowly, moving as Beatrice's hands guided. She was able to keep herself above the battles of her own body. She concentrated on making Beatrice come. She willed her to come loudly. Yes, my quiet blue librarian love, I wanted loud and long. And you came that way. Very loud for a very long time. Beatrice Lane, severe blue librarian, was actually screaming. Beatrice Lane, no longer in the tailored blue jacket, was screaming and crying louder than the loudest boy leaving the quiet library. Beatrice Lane screamed and raved and spilt herself shuddering as Daisy's fingers then her hand pressed in further and further.

Her hand was streaming with Beatrice's wetness, the bed was pungent with Beatrice's smell, the room in shock from Beatrice's screams. Thank goodness it was Sunday and the children were away.

Daisy's hand was soaked, the bed suddenly soaked too, she wanted to taste her wetness, taste it everywhere. There was no time for her to shift positions. Beatrice was making her come with her as she came again. Another sheet would have to hit the washing machine later, Daisy thought triumphantly. Her screams are mine. Mine are hers. I hear them. They fade. No thoughts. They were both smiling. Both sweating with desire, the stained sheet, hot and crumpled, beneath them. One of them had said, "Do the neighbours ever notice and wonder at our persistent cleanliness with our one Habitat brown sheet? Maybe we should buy a second." Did the thought occur that they might not ever again need a second sheet?

Drift with it. Fly with it. Fall into it. Steady. Don't let go of her. Keep your head steady so she turns on your hand. Thrusts against it. Away from it. Magnetic. She *has* to twist back on it. It dissolves. I dissolve. I feel what I do to her in my cunt. In my head. Lock. Twist. Turn. Key. Fit. Bone. Press bone. It slides. We slide. No one else in the whole damn judgemental world ever makes me feel this way.

Yes that was how it was Daisy thought, gripping hard on to the typewriter keys, her eyes filling with tears. No-one else.

Go back. Feel that way back. Go back in. Back and in. I slip in again, deep into her and move for her to thrust into me. My clitoris and hers circle on hands. Arch on fingertips. Head circles. Her clit is mine. I breathe "My clit. My clit. Come ON. Come ON." A hand is over my mouth. I want to lie back and be suffocated. I am helpless and powerful. She hears. Her pink moistness showing through black hairs responds. She makes sounds. Tongues. Then words. "I want to FUCK you."Violence beneath the joy. Joy in the violence. Shut ears to sounds. My sounds. Her sounds. Keep moving. Know what I do even as I begin again. Edge in sight but too pleasurable, too painful, to let myself be swept over. Stop. Don't stop. Stop. Don't stop. Screw me. Screw me. I say it to her. She loves it, eats it up. No stopping now. You great fuck. You great, great fuck. Strange to hurl into our rushing, to toss savagely within it, yet to be above the tossing. Inside. Outside. Both bodies alarmed, exhausted, by clever planning fingers which know exactly the spots, never miss the points for pleasure.

Difficult to write this without recalling and wanting her here now. Wanting to splatter her cool blue beauty with red and orange heat right across my neat white carpeted floor. Want her down, want her down on that floor, on a Saturday night, with the sounds of all the machines in the world screaming like her screams in my ice white workroom, only minutes before Ben's arrival. Just like that night aeons ago when they had made furious love on the old brown and white carpet recovering themselves only minutes before Charlie, Deborah and Beth's arrival back from their fathers!

The children. The children and Ben. Grown people all three of them. Even Nicola, the youngest, has slid into a well paid media job and seldom visited. Daisy took a deep breath, pulled herself back from the past, and thought about those she still cared for. Neither Deborah nor Charlie took her relationship with Benedict Quirk seriously though they had nothing against him. Beth quietly ignored him. Charlie in fact had met Ben at college, had once been quite friendly with him. Today Charlie was dully indifferent to everything to do with Daisy and Ben, resenting them both.

Deborah, a sensitive young woman, and Nicola, a fierce young feminist, with an acute grasp on the new ideology would not think well of Daisy's immersion into lust. Past or present. It was lesbian erotica or spiritual engagement nowadays and the words had moved on, matched up. But there you have it kids, Daisy said to herself, smiling. Twenty years ago, when we first met, it was fucking and screwing and when we did it at forty we hoped Deborah and Beth and Charlie and Nic were getting themselves a good education. Beatrice and I were. Education with Dynamic Sound! She slid her hand round the smooth loved body of the tape recorder that had played such an integral part of those years. Holding on to the machine her mind slipped away from the children and back to that Sunday.

Daisy had wanted her on any floor, in any field, in any bed, particularly a bed that wasn't theirs, (had they tried a children's bunk, or was that just one of their jokes?) in railway carriages, on buses, dangerously, ecstatically, in cars driven too fast. Often across the breakfast table, remembering last night, or at the tea table speculating silently about the next night. Each of them had been able to rip each other's clothes off with just their eyes meeting across the table. As the children ate fish fingers and mash, they drank a slow glass of red wine and made each other wet and fierce as they gazed steadily across at each other.

"Sometimes Bea, you look at Mummy real funny, in a funny way," Nic had once said perceptively. "What are you trying to tell Mummy that you don't want us to know?" The elder children laughed. Nic was known for her curiosity. Did the others know? Did they know that Daisy wanted her anywhere? Everywhere. Everytime. From the first day at that Conference. Was that why the last Sunday was no cooler nor stranger than those that had come before? Passion was never the problem, any more than was love.

They had made love for hours. Sometimes one of them resisting, sometimes the other. What Daisy remembered, gloated over even, was when Beatrice suddenly stopped resisting. Gave in quite suddenly. Shouting the words that turned them both on. Daisy knew she would have come sooner, more steadily, if she had gone into her vagina. That was the easy way. But she did not. Beatrice came the hard way. Sweating. She rarely sweated. Face twisting. Beautiful face not beautiful now. Real face. Real force. In everything that mattered Beatrice could be trusted to come the hard way, the necessary way, despite her love of ease and comfort. That was what Daisy admired most about her.

It was later. "That was extraordinary," Beatrice had said. Eyes shining. A quizzical grin at the edges of her mouth. She was almost back to looking beautiful and cool. She had been ugly with fierceness when she came. Not often I see her like that. Strong and unprotected. A different kind of beauty. No mask. Passion with her comforts, not distorts. She is encircled with disguises. Onion rings of pretence. Perhaps her cool beauty is another screen. To look as she looks most days, the days she gets lustful looks from other people, you have to appear serene, disinterested. You have to challenge people to wreck you with loving. The calm is only her surface.

The day before that particular Sunday, preparing for a science project in the library, she had told Daisy about surface tensions. Demonstrated how to break them. It made loving that Sunday memorable. First her tension, hatred, resentment, then tearing apart in hysteria. Frightened. Small. Then opening wide in desire. Lusting for it. Followed by enormous tenderness, then peace. Daisy's fear of destruction over. Hers too. A temporary closeness. Already Daisy was listening to the words just out of hearing. Already she was charting the changes in their life. Mapping out responses. Hardening herself. She lay next to Beatrice and knew then they would come, there would be small alteration after small alteration, compromising their life together. But for the moment they lay motionless. Beatrice looked tranquil, and because of that she looked like her photos.

On consideration, black and white *were* always the best. Beatrice liked them the best. She always said her beauty was a trial, an impediment. But the day they had their passport photos taken in the Post Office photo booth, and hers came out ugly she snatched them out of Daisy's hand and tore them up.

When Beatrice had flown to Thailand, had she still been vain? Had she still been a woman cool on the outside and raw and immoderate within? The postcards from exotic places don't tell you those facts. Not even that last one, the one from Thailand, had given Daisy much insight. It was a photo of the complex canal system in Bangkok where the markets front the water's edge. People were scurrying through the markets, looking busy and happy. Had Beatrice been amongst them? Had she been happy? The card offered Daisy no clues. She would have to rely on her memories.

Photographers can hint at the truth, if the sitter allows. Writers can play around with ideas that suggest it. But, Daisy sharply reminded herself, professionals are not supposed to play around. Professionals mean business. Writing was her business. The way she paid her mortgage on the new white house. The house with no room for blue memories, the house with no brown or orange cushions, no brown or orange blazing bedsitting room; the neutral toned writer's residence where with cold calculation a fifty-six year old professional woman earned a reasonable living.

Waited reasonably, between chapters, for a man of twenty-eight. There was no longer anything unreasonable in Daisy's narrow life. Nearly ten years of living without Beatrice, living alone, struggling with the words, had finally seen to that.

To write now about Beatrice she would have to take it seriously. Obtain a large advance. Make some royalties from it.

She would rather have taken her photograph.

She looked again at her watch, then at the large calendar on the white wall. Tomorrow was Remembrance Sunday. It was a good time to commemorate the dead. For a second, she shrank back from the sound of the word.

Dead. In the six months since the news of the plane crash she had not been able to use it. A cold November Saturday night was a reasonable time to start. She began to type fast and efficiently.

Ben would be there to take care of Sunday.

He had been caretaking for some time now. Five weeks after the news had been broken to Daisy, Ben had come to visit her. He had brought her some of Beatrice's possessions. Letters and tapes, several albums of photos. It was the first time she had met him. He was still bandaged, still badly scarred. But as he said, lucky to be alive. He was one of the only three survivors of the crash.

That is if you did not count Daisy.

THE REMOVAL

The couple lived together for seven years. Lovingly. Passionately. Tenderly. The couple lived in this house for seven years. Together. Two adults brought up four children together for seven years. Comfortably. Caringly. Committedly. Four children lived in this house for seven years. Together. With two adults.

The bodies and hearts of two adults and four children lived safely in this house. Time passed. Slowly. Securely. Inexorably. Seven years' time passed. (Times past. Ah, times past.) Slowly. Securely. Inexorably.

There had been no talk of moving. Or removing. Removal men had not been mentioned.

Then one day, you removed your body. Smoothly. Quickly. Cleanly. No festering. No blood. (None that drips anyway.) You have removed your body. But left your heart. You say. Reassuringly. Tactfully. Swiftly. As I move into your body space. As I move to hug you.

It is not an amputation.

It is change.

Love always changes.

With time.

Imperceptibly. Invisibly. Inevitably.

Love changes time. That time's past. (Ah, times past.) Time changes the past. Time passes. Imperceptibly. Invisibly. Inevitably.

You have removed your body. Smoothly. Cleanly. Quickly. No damage done. No wounds. (None that won't heal anyway.) You have removed your body. I still have your heart. You say. Kindly. Patiently. Distantly. As you move into another room.

It is not consequential.

It is time. (Time for it to happen.)

Time changes love.

Times change.

Invisibly. Imperceptibly. Irrevocably.

Love changes time. That time's past. (Ah, times past.) Time changes the past. Times pass. Invisibly. Imperceptibly. Irrevocably.

You have removed your body. Smoothly. Quickly. Cleanly. No need for words. No needs. I have no needs. (None that glare anyway.) Love is not merely bodies. Love is the heart. You say. Placatingly. Tolerantly. Impatiently. As you move into another bed.

It is not burglary.

It is not a loan.

(Due back. Due time.)

You have lent your body.

Passionately. Sensually. Indiscreetly.

To the woman inside this house. To the woman inside our room. To the woman inside our bed.

Inside this house. Inside my tomb. Inside my head. I remove your body. Skilfully. Smoothly. Dispassionately. I saw it up. Limb from limb.

Later they remove your body. Coldly. Clinically.

Professionally. No expense spared. No need. (Your estate will pay anyway.)

The woman and I watch silently. Then one of us tidies away the heart. The other minds the children.

ELEANOR'S CASTLE

There are four newly sharpened pencils in the white plastic tray on the desk in the Third Bedroom in Eleanor's Castle. I notice that Eleanor has thoughtfully left a Mars automatic sharpener for the pencils. She herself uses old razor blades. I wonder if this says something significant about the way we each write and draw. I look pensively at the two pencil drawings above the bed. More traditional than Eleanor's present style which is for large poster-bright paintings.

Sharpen one of the pencils. Take off the sweatshirt. Hot in Eleanor's Castle. It had been hot in the pub too.

Relive the evening. Small noisy Irish pub. The Jig and Saw. One of her old haunts. It had been a benefit social for striking factory workers. Lots of well-intentioned Liberals. Several ex-Communist Party members. Eleanor of course knows most of them. "Some of them I haven't seen since the old Party days," she says, grinning happily. Her idea to support the social. "It will do you good, Daisy, to leave the typewriter. Get out for once. Widen your circle. Support a few mixed causes." But the real reasons for going are hers.

Each time she returns from the gruelling trip to

Edinburgh, no matter how tired she is, she throws herself frantically into local politics, feminism, anti-war activities. Her other life. The dark side to her drawings.

(Think of the new book....I could make Hermione a Communist as well as an artist. Allow her politics rather than her creativity to dominate the book. Too close to home? Maybe...)

Watch Eleanor mingle with the crowds in the pub. Tall. Graceful. Impossibly striking with that mass of red hair. Tousled and messy. Strides about with an air of authority. Sense of style. Watch her talking excitedly. Her excitement rich. Feverish. Catching.

(Catch me. Catch me. I whisper. But only to myself.)

She stops to talk earnestly to the two male musicians. The lanky guitarist gives her an affectionate hug. Several women are braving an Irish jig. I join Eleanor in a noisy shouting ring round the women. "Ten years ago I'd have been up there dancing, Daisy. But not now." She puts her arm idly round my shoulders. We both laugh as we recognise the truth of her statement.

Forty-two sits easily upon her. But once again there are dark rings under her eyes. The Edinburgh run is taking its toll. Some of us have tried to lift the strain but there is not much we can do.

Follow her with my eyes as she strolls from group to group. She wears one of her son Jake's cheap black sweatshirts as if she'd acquired it at Harrods.

(Pull her back into my book.... Should Hermione have a similar panache? Think not. Somehow already see her as eternally moving. Perpetual motion, constant action. Concerned with speed not with appearance. Dressed in cheap windswept cagoules. Autumn colours, falling leaves, scattered pages, shaking trees.)

Eleanor chats and laughs with the men, then settles contentedly with a bunch of women, crowded together on too few seats. She talks first to one woman, then to another, making each feel special. Important. Bathed in her light. She uses her hands excitedly as she talks. Long slim white fingers still marked with paint. She has been working for several days on a gaudy four foot high abstract. Determined to have it ready to show Lydia. "Not that Lydia will appreciate it. She doesn't understand most of my pictures and doesn't like what she does understand." Eleanor didn't sound worried. Strong and confident within her own framework, criticism seldom touches her. "Lydia's indifference doesn't bother me, Daisy," she said reading my thoughts. "We do share other vital things. What bothers me more is how much Jake dislikes Lydia, how temperamental he is about her. Still I daresay he will get over it."

Most of what they share these days are the long drawn out painful weeks of Lydia's illness. I do not say that aloud. Nor do I remind her of the early unnerving period during Charlie and Beth's hostility to me. They did however get over it. Eventually. Perhaps Eleanor is right not to worry. In the pub Eleanor makes another recovery. Gesticulates wildly to drive a point home. Once or twice brushes her hand through the red wiry hair. A short head of hair on top of a long elegant body. Out of place, like a scarlet lavatory brush.

The crowds thin. The music dies down. Back finally to Eleanor's Castle. Tucked away tidily in a quiet road near the station. Into the warm cosy kitchen. Untidy as always. Past Jake, skulking over the television in the sitting room. Jake's red hair the same screaming shade as his mother's but worn long, straggly, short on top with a single red braid, plaited inefficiently, streaming behind him. Fourteen, streetwise, brusque and often hostile to Lydia. Jake is a softie where it doesn't show. Beth and Charlie and Little Nic still at home with me, even though their mother has left.

The girls will be happier with you, Daisy. They've always been happy with you, Beatrice had said. (You're wrong, you're wrong, they were happy with both of us. Don't say it. Keep it. Change it. Write it differently later.)

Eleanor puts the kettle on. Choice of herbals. Peppermint sounds healthy. I write you in my mind. Invent you as you move, scavenger amongst the pots and pans, looking for clean cups and spoons. I sit around happy to observe. Picking up crockery, picking up phrases, here and there. Words. Yours. "Been married, more or less, seventeen years. Now I think I want to live with a woman. Tried once, for a short time, and failed. Do not want to fail again." I know the woman. Fifteen years younger than Eleanor. Too much in love with her. Too obvious about it. Her failure too.

(For a split white second I envy the turbulent miracle of that failure. Know I, too, could want you like a fix.)

"Her failure too," I say, thinking aloud.

We perch on stools in the kitchen opposite each other. Close the connecting door between us and Jake. Close the connections.

"I think I could try with you, Daisy. Share a space. When I am not with Lydia of course."

"Of course." Say it easily. Know the routine.

"But you are known to be neat. Your own house is excruciatingly tidy. Even the kids don't seem to have the impact on it that Jake has on mine. Hope your neatness won't be a problem. Beatrice never found it a problem did she?"

(Beatrice had been neat herself. If only that had been the problem.)

"No that's not a problem." Reassurance comes fast. You shift cheerfully on your perch. Bring your stool closer to mine. I stir the peppermint tea round and round. I am waiting for the next line. Watching the red gold hair, harsh under the kitchen neon light.

"But I can't live with a woman I'm involved in, in that way. Of course it's got be someone I care about. Like you. But no uppers and downers. Know what I mean? Uppers and downers are not on."

Pause. Logical. Persuasive. "All the time and energy we invested in passion we could put into our drawing and writing. You know that Daisy…"

Yes I know that. What writer, what artist doesn't? Sensible. Sane. Agreed. Nod and smile.

(Save her lines in my mind for Hermione. Change the colour of her hair. Need she be quite so tall?)

We sip the green brew watching the steam coil. You start to say something. Hesitate. Then edge out: "I don't want to lose you, Daisy. Can't risk losing you." I listen to the words. Look at the tousled red hair. Clear words. Muddled hair. Want to straighten it out. Want to run my hands through your sentences. Over your head. Stroke the back of your neck. Gently under your shirt. Touch the red tangles, begin to untangle the sounds, begin to sound the. Tangle. Untangle. Tangle. Untangle. Brush up the phrases, brush down the tangles, touch up the lines, touch down the. Touch down.

The steady dark eyes are careful to hold me away.

Sit on my hands. My teacup is empty. Did Eleanor make a pot? Empty but the words spill out. Words. Mine. Spill over. Jerky. Unthinking. A flood. Like my love. "Eleanor, you are the only woman I want…want to go to bed with." I hang the words, shivering like catkins. Rustling. Very slightly. Their newness is terrifying. Years of friendship. Now these new stark words. Cloud messages. Harsh. Words that would be tolerable on paper. Could be altered. Softened. Rejigged. Punctuation added. The whole phrase obliterated if necessary.

Necessary. Long pause. Another risk. "It had to be said, Eleanor." Return to your eyes like a maze I cannot find my way out of. You do not answer. A dialogue that lasts for endless years. But you are not contributing. The silence is not hostile. No awkwardness. It did not have to be said. Point had long ago been taken. Overkill.

"Do not use sledgehammer. Do not close down the possibilities."

Those words over my typewriter. Words Bea used about my writing. Your words I retained when you left your work and went away. Left the drawings. Left Jake. Alone in the Castle. Went to Edinburgh. To Lydia. "I'm not in love with Lydia. It's not sexual passion. But it is total security. Absolute commitment." Lydia ill.

"I want you to remember, Daisy, that I am effectively married to her." Those words before the illness had taken hold.

(Now Lydia dying of leukaemia. Disease complicating your love for her, my love for you.)

"If Lydia lives after Jake has left home, I intend to go to Scotland, to be with her. If necessary permanently. But I know I shall still need a space here. Must have my own space to work, to draw. I think I could share that space with you, Daisy."

Check statements. Own space. Known to be neat. Space out the words. Neaten up thoughts. Relax. Steady the rhythm. Cool the conversation. There is time. It is Lydia who is ill. Lydia who matters. Jake turns up the television next door. Chat over tea and biscuits. Relatively fresh. Biscuits. Biscuit tin lid doesn't fit properly. Dreadful television programme. Expect the girls are watching it at home. Forgot to tell them I was leaving early tomorrow. Too late now to ring home. Begin to worry about the time. About Deborah and the other three. The train goes at six thirty am. Must be up at least an hour before that. Shall not be able to phone the girls then either. Far too early. Eleanor puts her arms around me. Hugs me tightly. "We are both tired," she says reading my thoughts. "It's anxiety born of fatigue, Daisy. The girls will be fine."

We wash up together. Dirty rings on some cups. Perhaps a spot of bleach. Perhaps a spot of bother. Rings on most of the cups. Rings on most of her fingers. Large amethyst stone on the middle finger of the left hand. A purple knuckle duster. Streaks of red paint. On the other hand silver rings. Only silver rings. One on each finger. *(Stroke me. Take off the rings and stroke me.)*

"Will you be alright in the Third Bedroom, pet?"

"Of course I shall be alright. You know I like that room."

It is going to be alright. I trust her. But do not lose me, lady, because I trust you enough to be explicit. Fresh eggs plicit. This is the Year of the Bristol Diet. No choice. The diet has had miraculous results with the victims of leukaemia. No meat. Wholefoods only. Wholewords only. No battery phrases. No fenced in language. No Es in vocabulary. No additives in speech. No frozen nouns or preserved adjectives. I come to you freshly, lady. I and my words. Visible clean corrections every time. Throwing caution to the. Taking risks. Risking takes.

(Take off the rings. Take off the rings and run your fingers through my tidy phrases. Mess them up. Fling them about. Take off the rings. Take off. Take me. Take me and untidy me. Taking her. Entering her.)

Upstairs to bed. Correction. Come clean. Wholewords only on the Bristol plan. Beds. I am in the Third Bedroom. Between you and Jake. He is still downstairs lolling in front of the box. Raggedy red hair falling out of the single plait. Do all teenagers today retire later than their mothers?

I could have rung the girls if I'd thought of it earlier. What kind of a mother am I? Reliable? Unreliable? (Mother? Substitute?) Eleanor comes in to say goodnight. "Stop worrying, Daisy, the girls are OK and they are certainly not worrying about you."

Everything in the Third Bedroom of Eleanor's Castle for the insomniac writer. White typing fluid. A4 paper. Several 4B pencils. The automatic sharpener. More than one dictionary. Two of Eleanor's drawings on the wall. Several modern poems. Everything except you Eleanor. You are asleep next door. Safer to assume you are asleep. Tongued to search you out. Find out where you are. Little by little finding out. Filling out. Fill. Overwhelm. Waiting the other's tongue. Finding you. I want the time to find you out. Time among the plants measured in terms of space. Time to stroke you, time to touch you, inscribe you with my words and hold you. The feel of you in my hands. Almost certainly forever determined. Lydia's disease means we cannot determine anything. Can only wait. Keep the trust. The wise will polish their lamps and wait.

Hard to sleep in the third strange bed.

Set the computer alarm for five thirty am. The girls bought the clock for me last Christmas. Push the button to snooze function. Pick a particularly obnoxious tune to awaken to. Excitement sweeps across me. Must be away sharp in the morning. Back to the North. The pre-Christmas trek to old friends, some of them old lovers. Tonight you are asleep in the front room of Eleanor's Castle. You need all the sleep you can get. Shall not ask you to drive me. Cabs are fast. I shall leave you sleeping. You are tired from the constant travelling. Tired from fighting the disease. Tired from fighting with Jake. Jake always angry about Lydia. You do not need any more fights Eleanor.

You need me as your friend. And I? I do not want to lose you either. Cannot afford more losses this year. Still awake. Get water from bathroom. Notice scales. Cannot resist checking weight. Lost four pounds. Can afford that loss. Who would have thought the old woman had so much vanity still in her? So much vanity, so much blood. Blood, ruby clean blooms. Sweet blood berries. Would suck even your blood while you imagined magical lines. Want you that much. Blood spiralling a wreath of crimson roses. Wet. Blood red. Desperately impossible desires. Stick to the possible.

"Writing makes you impossible to live with, Daisy." Finally the girls' mother had said it.

"I make a fair living by the writing now," I'd pleaded. (Don't go, don't go, the girls need you, I need you. Don't say it. Don't say anything. Keep it. Check it. Change it. Write it later.)

"We don't share living together any more, Daisy, we only share your writing. It is no longer possible, Daisy. No longer plausible for us to continue in this house. You have stopped been reasonable." Beatrice was calm. Do not say anything. Stick to the possible.

Stand on the scales in the bathroom of the Castle, three doors away from you, naked and bedwarm. Check emotions on the bathroom scales. The machine must be inaccurate. What it registers is hardly plausible. What I feel is hardly reasonable. That is the problem with reality. Too unreasonable. Do a rewrite. Easier to manipulate fiction. Safer to stick to what you know.

"You turn all of our lives into fiction, Daisy. It no longer feels safe."

Buy Eleanor a new pair of bathroom scales. It simply is not fair on unwary houseguests to have such inaccurate measuring tools. Give them a tap. Check feelings again. Do I still live by their definitions? Calculate even my emotions on their measures? On what scale do I measure passion? Correction. Passion is not on the agenda this year. No uppers and downers. Back to the Third Bedroom. Pick up the first sharpened pencil. 4B. Soft. Sensuous. Strange that I do not know what Eleanor uses to correct her drawings. Art is the most private part of her life. Sit for a long time. So little control in all of our situations this year. Gain control with a 4B. It will write softly but firmly for miles.

"You have to get mileage out of every situation, Daisy. Living with you has become data for writing."

Living is data for writing. Writing is one reason for living. Possible to live with? Impossible to live with? Possible, impossible, cannot afford any more losses this year. Stick to the writing. Stick to the Third Bedroom. All artists lie. You know that Eleanor. Do not know you well enough. Years of knowing lie ahead. Do not risk that knowledge, do not risk those years. Risk. Eyes close. Hands move slowly through the dark finding where you bedwarm are. This is more than indiscriminate desire. This is more than caring. This is more than words we do not mention. This is. Time among the plants.

★ ★ ★ ★

Dawn. Saturday morning. Five am. The alarm goes every seven minutes. High tech snooze function painfully operative. Break eyelids open. Dress sharply. *("Daisy is a sharp dresser," the girls said last week.)* Make the bed. Not much to make. Hardly lain in. Don't lay anything on my bed. Don't lay anything on my words. Downstairs. Quietly past Jake's room. Curtains still drawn in the sitting room. Through to the kitchen. Feel clumsily for the kettle. Cab will be here in fifteen minutes. Plot my route. Kettle off.

Coffee. Spoon it. Carefully. Measured grains, measured thoughts. Should be no coffee in a Bristol plan kitchen. Should be all shipshape and Bristol fashion. Coffee is a big killer. Leukaemia is a big killer. Thoughts dismissed. Left right, left right, left right. Ten shun. Tension must be paid. Forster? Miller? But look what happened to Marilyn Monroe. All that attention. Still not enough. All she had at the last was that beautiful body. Beautiful bodies do not last. Beautiful. Body. Hers. At last. Think it. Dark softness in her room upstairs. Catch breath. Small open lipped breath. Hot and hold her. Hold her tight, never let her go. Steam from kettle. Pour. Linger over the coffee. Linger over the thought of her. Near. Inaccessible. Removed. Rumpled. Short rumpled and raggedy red hair. An inappropriate brush. Ginger, gold, bristling. Ginger gold, everywhere. Long white fingers. Ginger gold and red paint stains. The feel of her long fingers. Long to feel her fingers. Long to feel her fingers feel for me. Dry the cup. Tidy the place up. (Known to be neat.) Cut the loaf. Straighten the edges. Bread hard. No lid on the bin. A moment's irritation. Look everywhere. Cannot see the lid. The kitchen is streaming with ginger gold hair. Perhaps Eleanor and Jake do not have a lid for the breadbin. Perhaps they do not notice when the bread gets stale. Wash up Jake's supper plate. Put the tomato ketchup away. Grin. Think of the girls.

Scan watch. Six minutes to go. Slowly up the stairs. Pause on the fifth stair. Only need two minutes with her. Cannot afford to spend longer. Cannot afford to spend my whole life. Downstairs again. Sturdy independent steps. Stop casually at the bookshelves. Over them Eleanor's drawings. On them my poems. Your pictures are hard and bright. Your pictures do not come easy. Come instead. Want that. Want that fiercely. Want you when you drift back from the bathroom carelessly zipping up your bright red jeans. I nestle in the space between the zippers. Want you hard and wet when you telephone to talk prosaically about the words or the grocery trip or the children or to tell me how difficult the day's drawings have been. Will you always draw the hard way? Will you always come the hard way? With lines and spaces. There are lines we do not draw and do not say, you and I. Sometimes speech has restricted function.

Run a trained eye along the bookshelves. Other women's poems. Mainly modern like those on the wall of the Third Bedroom. Take down Alice Notley.

"Mornings I wonder if I can fill my stocking. By evenings I wish I weren't so in love."

Quite so, Notley. Of course I don't wear stockings. Of course I'm not in love. I don't know anyone who does wear stockings. Or anyone who is. In love.

Illusions. They are just necessary illusions. They hold women up like suspenders.

Upstairs again, two at a time. High with held-in excitement like Jake and the girls at Christmas. Careful. Must not wake Jake. Slip very quietly into the front room. Your room. Darkness. Cannot see. Cannot see anything. Know where you are. Feel. No words. At last, no words. Bare. Do not chart it. Do not record it. This time no camera eye, no tape ears. Do not allow it. Try to want only what is possible. Try not to want your impossibly dangerous drawings. Aim for the ordinary. Humdrum. Run of the mill. Stick to our steady friendship. The sharing of mothering. The strength of our work. This friendship has hardly begun to reach its prime. Still in training. Stages, always stages. Test these stages first. Settle for the growing unspoken bonds. We are moving inexorably without trying. Settle for these good possibilities.

These bonds last. Passion will evaporate. Nestlé's evaporated passion. Want that too. Want you all milky and warm. Fix the attention. Fix. Want you like a fix. Echoes of the past. But the future is more and different. Other and else. Hold me, hold me. Cancelled.

Recall Eleanor's words in the Castle kitchen: "Instinct. It goes back to my riding mistress. Some of us feel it, some of us don't."

Some of us feel it now, wet with waiting. Desire to reach the unspoken. Then suddenly the dark holding you. Touching your bare shoulders. My hand feeling for your breast. Your arms around me. Want to lose myself in your time. Where I am now, language has limited use, and you using it, murmuring sleepily: "Have a safe journey up north, Daisy. Have a good time with your friends." Holding me tight as you talk. Utter darkness. Me using it: "Thanks. Take care. See you when I get back."

Me not using it. Touch me. Unfold me. Enfold me. Somewhere a wild cry.

"Hope the results of Lydia's scan are OK, Eleanor. Hope Lydia is a little better. Give her my good wishes. Have a relaxing time in Edinburgh if you can."

Time. Time among the plants is measured in. Bricks and mortar. Chestnut trees. Hopes for the future. Lines from the present. "I was married for seventeen years….I am effectively married to Lydia…It makes me very secure…I do not want to fail again…No uppers or downers…Need my own space…"

The space that they occupy little by little filling out.

(Fill out Hermione. Leave her the space. Feed Hermione into the word processor. Let the machine remember Hermione.)

"It has a 256K Memory," I had said proudly to Beatrice. The man in the computer shop said it will store 256 thousand characters including spaces. Always remember to count the spaces."

Spaces between her zipper. Nestle in those spaces. Golden red jeans. Golden red hair.

"Each disc is double sided, double density. We could share the dot matrix printer," I'd begged.

"Daisy, there is nothing left to share."

Dots placed after notes or rests increase their time value by half. Need to increase the time with you. Value the time with you. Time for rests. Time of notes. Time increases your value to me not only as the girls' mother but as a rock. Your value as my matrix, the rock in which gems are embedded, my rock, to be embedded in you. Want to be embedded in you.

"Words are a game with you, Daisy." Beatrice was ruffled. "You never stop making words out of words. The girls have caught the habit. Can't you play another game?"

It is not a game. It is a way of spelling words, it is a spell. I do not know how to cast a spell over you, I do not know what words to use with you, I do not want to use words with you, words are what you want.

Want what is reasonable. Share the words, share the lines, share the process, share even a house, keep to the Third Bedroom. Keep to anything to keep her.

Cannot afford more losses this year.

Hear the cab. Whisper goodbye. Let her go. Let go. Hold her tight and let her go.

At the railway station buy the inevitable postcards. If nothing else a reliable writer, reliable friend, reliable mother.

The fiction of reliability.

Dear Eleanor,

Thanks for the bed. Loved the poems on the walls, as always love the drawings. Just started a new novel.

Am calling it "Hermione's House". See you on return.
   Love, Daisy.

★ ★ ★ ★

The woman sitting on the London-Edinburgh Express was
deathly pale. Appeared exhausted, frail, seemed many years
older than her actual fifty-five years. She wore, however,
a calm and satisfied expression as she carefully reread the
first sixteen pages of the typed manuscript on her lap. She
sighed contentedly.

   The reliability of fiction.

   Yes, she thought, that would do as a conclusion to the
draft of the first chapter. There was, of course, still the
problem of the book's title. How would Hermione react to
the name of her house? It was certainly a possibility. She
shifted uncomfortably in her seat. The pains were again
very bad. The doctors had been very angry at her sudden
decision to leave Scotland and make the long journey south.
She knew in medical terms they were right. But she had
so much needed to be with her Companion, to see her for
once in her own setting, to show her the new book.

   All things considered, it had been a good weekend. Now
she was on her way home to Scotland. Possibly her last
journey. Now the thank you letter.

   Dearest Hermione,

   Thank you for a warm and restful time and as always your
constant ministering. I did not understand the poetry on
your wall and I still do not care for those overlarge gaudy
abstracts. I do however care a great deal for you, my dearest.
In this diseased time, you have become quite literally my
life's blood. I can say no more.

   I was glad you wanted me, at last, to meet your highly

political woman friend. We had more in common than you had predicted, although we were, needless to say, both a trifle wary.

Thank you for making those thoughtful comments about my manuscript. Writing it is helping me to fight and is a great support when you cannot be with me. I have now decided on a title. I rather think it will amuse you. It is to be called "Eleanor's Castle".

By the time of your next visit, I hope the manuscript will have progressed, as will have your beloved friend on this earth and beyond.

Your Lydia.

PAINTBOXED IN

T he studio is, as always, untidy. Your garish paints, ragged cloths, everywhere. Strips of light streak through the open window, falling on your easel. You shrug but not impatiently. Stand back as if to view the painting. You rub your hand up and down over the rough surface. Up and down. Up and down. Until you have memorised the picture by your touch. Reach blind and certain for the correct colour. You smell each tube of paint painstakingly.

You always know where to find what you want. I never do. What I want is not of course on today's agenda. My eyes flicker towards the stairs. I dare not speak. Steadily you work on, as the light slowly fades. I try to concentrate on my manuscript. Type neatly at my small desk in the darkest corner of the crowded room. Every page is numbered in my tiny black italic script.

I feel contained. There is space but no air between us.

You put down your paintbrush. Wash it carefully. You attend to every task carefully. Wipe it on the red-stained rag.

"Are you ready?" your voice says, but the eyes, green-flecked hooded eyes are still on the canvas. Or at least in that general direction. Give nothing away. You are not yet satisfied. I am ashamed how easily I am satisfied. How easily you satisfy me.

I type the last line. Close the pages. "Ready!" I say, trying to sound uninterested. Upstairs your eyes fasten on mine. You begin to use your hands.

You describe my body in colours. Vividly. Rapidly. No holds barred. No holes barred. Descriptive hands off and on. On and off. Pressing the paints in intimate places, colouring in the spaces.

"Are you ready?" your voice says. But the eyes, green-flecked now, are somewhere still on that canvas. You are not yet content. I have never known you content. You shame me with your industrious discontent. "Ready," I say, too eagerly, and begin to use my hands.

At the time I am quite uncomfortable. It is too picturesque. Too much colour everywhere. And no sounds. No words. Nothing to be seen, nothing to be said. I am a writer of prose. And cons. Deal in hard clear words. I don't mix meta. Fors or againsts. I don't mix colours. I am not a palette.

"I can't get it right," you breathe, getting it right. Just right. Come on, come on, don't stop now. The picture *you* mean. I should have known. Red is for stop. Green is for go. You turn away. Eyes on the open door. Don't go. Don't go. Green flecks in those eyes.

I stain easily though, when your fingers reach in and down. I colour the bed blood red.

I never was ready. I was waiting for you to finish the damn picture.

Later, in the studio, on the floor by the easel, still uncomfortably, I reach up for a rainbow I do not believe is there.

FRESH EVIDENCE

PART ONE

I t was not her courtroom.

At least not in the way the house was. Private domain. Under her control. Subject only to the austere charm of Evelyn's flawless taste. A restrained and gracious house, an Arctic atmosphere, ice blue decor, classical and cold like the decisions she took.

"Of course you share it Nick," she had said. The young, the young that you suddenly find you love, need constant reassurance.

Another lie about the young, Evelyn told herself severely, brushing small beads of moisture back under the wig.

The young do not need anything. They do not need you for a start.

Irritably, Evelyn pushed away this train of thought as irrelevant. She was a martinet about correct thoughts for correct settings. Courtrooms demanded an orderly mind. They were the fitting backdrop for the lucid systematic intelligence of the woman Evelyn had trained herself to be.

A woman who would list her weaknesses, tabulate her assets, and chart such unruly emotions as could not be reduced, entered and itemised onto a small blue file index card.

Evelyn, who did not believe God sat in the judgement seat to ensure that all was right with the world, did however firmly believe in the dustmen coming on Wednesdays as a routine that staved off insanity.

The decorum and discipline of this grey-voiced terrain of rectitude allowed her to feel at ease. Even though it was not HER courtroom. Public domain. Open to all. Hall of justice. Arena for fair play. Seat of comparative wisdom.

At this patently nonsensical notion, Evelyn shifted uncomfortably on the bench. She could hear Nick's strong ringing laughter. She did not want to hear the clear radical viewpoint of youth. She had quite enough problems dealing with the somewhat muddier one that went with middle age.

Blurred edges how they disturbed her.

Edging now into her mind, blurring her vision, the disturbing sight of Nick dazzling in the cerise pink shirt, unbuttoned across the chest, aroused by the early morning tension, flaring up, swinging those long untidy legs across her immaculately tidy bed. The strength in the relentlessly moving legs matched by the fury in the remorselessly cutting sentences.

"Don't give me that! Of course it's your house! Everyone knows that. Like everything else in this life we are supposed to share, it belongs to you."

Their last morning together in the house. Her house. Before she had decided Nick should leave. (Was it she who had made that decision?)

Evelyn tried to concentrate. Fixed her eyes on the defendant. A plain young woman very poorly dressed in an ill-fitting navy suit wearing a grey haunted expression.

Her eyes, a shade lighter than the unfashionable steely blue, flickered nervously from side to side. There was a milky white stain on the skirt above beige tights one of which was wrinkled. Evelyn felt an irritating desire to straighten up the left tight. It did not after all take much to neaten oneself up for a court appearance.

She did not need Nick's biting admonitions to tell her she was being unfair.

The defendant had stolen eight pairs of trousers from one shop and sixteen cotton shirts from two other shops. Two shirts for each pair of pants, Evelyn thought idly, save on the washing, not a bad scheme. After all, the woman had a great many children, there must be a great deal of washing. The defence had let slip that all the stolen trousers and shirts were colour co-ordinated. The young woman had obviously taken the Mix and Match injunction seriously.

Evelyn looked at her with a new respect. Then with a certain curiosity. To steal well-orchestrated ensembles had an air of deftness belied by the woman's clumsy ill-fitting look as if she and her suit had somehow been scrambled together. Something did not match up.

An intriguing sense of style attached to the felony that was not evident from, indeed was at odds with, the random dishevelled appearance of the felon. Had the woman deliberately dressed down for today's performance in court? Evelyn was sure it *was* a performance. She looked again at the young woman's face. There were dark smudges under the eyes. Tear marks, or perhaps cleverly achieved stale makeup.

She heard the defence counsel reiterate the terrible state of the woman's poverty, her inability to care adequately for her five children, the fact that she had been beaten up and then abandoned by her alcoholic husband. Evelyn's sympathies were not aroused. She had heard it all before. It was not the young woman's first appearance in court. There was always work to be had if you were not congenitally lazy. You did not have to resort to systematic stealing.

"How could you prosecute a woman in that situation?" Nick's compelling clarity. Impetuous, headstrong, resolute, ardour breaking into flames, all the sturdy righteousness of youth.

"How can you be content to use all your training and all your skills for such patently unjust purposes? In all these years why have you never used your damn legal mind to help those that really need your help? People who haven't had your education, your expensive long-winded training, who've never been offered a chance. Oh what's the point......The easy way you wield the purse strings makes it impossible for you to understand!"

The young one's scorn was everywhere. Filling her head, filling the crowded courtroom. Scathing sounds exploded in her mind discharging sparks of moral venom, the same angry words that had been hurled the morning before Nick's departure. The same contemptuous phrases that had hurtled across the bedroom too many mornings recently. Making a departure a necessity.

What right had Nick, Nick of all people, to say that? Now she too was furious. Bursting with the sentences she had swallowed back over brimming bowls of natural low fat yoghurt, choking on the chopped nuts, anxious to get away, determined not to be late for court; Nick insistent on half-baked words and rolls, spread thinly with Swiss yeast pâté. Their temperatures rising like the oven.

What was wrong with Sainsbury's unreconstructed marmalade? What was wrong with the fact that she earned a decent living?

Compromise and additives were an integral part of any

career structure. It was her job. It was her job. It was a good job. Where the hell would Nick be without that job, without her professionalism, without her ease with the purse strings?

Under cover of the black gown, Evelyn, black with fury, felt for the two folded brown envelopes with the week's cash in them. Suddenly she made up her mind. She had had enough of recriminations, of endless conversations about power trips, of wearying discussions about who was controlling whose life.

It was not going to be an easy lunch.

She went back over the evidence. Carefully sorted it. Came, as she always came, to a reasonable decision. This relationship, it seemed, could not be changed, the rational answer therefore was to a call a recess.

Lunchtime today was as good or as bad as any other mealtime. It was after all the refection when the brown envelopes changed hands. Today's collation, at a more modest restaurant than usual, would not be an inappropriate occasion. The issue could be resolved before the pudding.

The defence was summing up.

"The defendant has had a particularly difficult childhood. Not enough attention was paid to her. The mother was always absent. The father dissolute and drunk."

Evelyn's mind strayed back years. The Disorderly Days. The days of turbulent slipshod living with Ted and the baby. An outbreak of car machinery and nappies in the one anarchic bedsitting room. No order anywhere. The child crying. The child always crying. How could she be expected to study against a boring backdrop of howls? Babies bored her even more than they bored Ted. Ted's baby bored her more than most. Hard to believe it was her baby too.

Where was Ted? She had only ten minutes before she had to leave for Chambers. Distaste for the child's squalls was overtaken by fury at Ted's unpunctuality. Ted would be as conscious of the time as she was, and as stubbornly enraged, awareness and anger increasing his determination not to leave the pub until the last possible moment. The pub was certainly where he was. Evelyn knew that, even if she could not point a precise finger at the location of today's hostelry.

During the Disorderly Days, she spent her time studying, he spent his boozing with his raucous mates from the car factory. Bright himself but in her eyes impossibly wilful he had given up his engineering training and had taken a well-paid job as a car mechanic.

"Someone has to pay for *your* bloody studies," he would say, new resentment overtaking ancient pride, well intentioned whisky slurring his speech.

Time and drink running out. Not enough money. Not enough care. The child crying. The child always crying.

"A particularly difficult childhood. Attention must be paid. Not enough pay. Not enough attention. The mother always absent. The father dissolute and drunk."

Only in the huge unmade bed did they occasionally stop battling, iron out dissensions between ever rumpled sheets. The child crying. The child always crying. How could they be expected to love against a boring backdrop of howls?

"It's your turn, it's your turn," she breathed, her voice soft. His rasping. Hot. Slipping. "It's you the child needs little darlin'." Not now, not now. It's you. It's you. Crying, always crying, a different kind of crying, wet, slipping, my turn, come on, come, you, you.

Late she would be late. Struggling to get up. Dressing. Later, later, touching her breast, trying to retain her, a drop of car grease sliding onto her clean Paisley blouse. "Let go," she said, wrenching free.

Let go. Let go of the memories. Let the past go. Deal

with the present. With Nick who had too eagerly rushed to take Ted's place centre stage in Evelyn's crowded life. It was time to let Nick go too.

It would not be an easy lunch.

"Tell me about your memories of your childhood, Nick," she had prodded. Knowing it all. Knowing it all from before. There had been other loves after Ted. None as young as Nick. "Let me in," she had wheedled. "Tell me the bits I do not know." Her eyes sharp. Keen observer's eyes. Ready for action. It was night time. She wore her daily pavement eyes.

"Tell me, tell me," Nick teased. "Offer you the evidence. Wait for you to sift it. Watch you try to be impartial. CAN you be impartial? There must be some evidence you are partial too…"

Nick smiling at her. Nick's fingers, long slender fingers adorned by two heavy gold signet rings, stroked her hair. The rings, the rings that could no longer be worn on that hand. Evelyn smiled back. Happy. Feeling incredibly comfortable. A day without a row. Breakfast without a clash. They had driven to the quiet restaurant in the market place where they could eat undisturbed. Beige suede walls. Fresh freesias on each table. Cream on the other tables. Pink on theirs. A restaurant where you paid for privacy and certain select touches. Peace and Henri's French cooking at a moderate price. Lunch had been easy that day.

She turned her wandering glance back to the Defence. Counsel was a bald man with ginger whiskers. "Not your sort, lovely. Not your sort at all!" She could hear Nick mock. A smile lightened her face. What was her sort? Had Ted ever been her sort? Hardly. A wry grin as she remembered his large oily hand on her breast. Pulling her away from her brief. Briefly pulling her away. Pulling her back into the large messy bed. Messing her up. Making her late. In the ornate pink mirror oil and sweat reflections. Reflections of other times. Other beds. Rumpled sheets and car grease marks. The bed unmade hours later. Make it, why don't you make it? Fool, you crazy fool, I am trying to make it, make it with you, make you. Shut up about the bed. Shut up and love me.

No, not her sort.

For Ted, love was a label for extravagantly packaged and barely civilised lust. Can't we take lust neat? Do we have to use disguises? Ted lacked a clear intellect.

And Nick? Was Nick her sort? Probably not. Although there was a superficial agreement. Occasional attempts at compromise. Even a rota for the chores. There are some things the young are more flexible about.

Nick needed politics to wrap up passion. Passion raw was unsound. Ideologically incorrect. Nick wanted to be a whole person, to have sex that was exciting, worthwhile and spiritually enhancing.

"You hate that phrase don't you? Not a sixties phrase at all!"

Evelyn had laughed and agreed. She did hate the phrase. How pure the young are. How temptingly pure.

Nick dressing at the end of her bed. Not messy now. Not messy at all. It had not been messy for eight years. Since Ted had left with that woman. Clean sheets. Clean nights. The vulgar (exotic Ted called it) pink mirror smashed into pieces the night Ted left. Evelyn, impartial, thorough, coldly detached, smashing the vulgar pink mirror in a frenzy of anger and humiliation. How could he have left her for a baby sitter? For the only baby sitter who failed to wash up properly, the only one who left grease marks in the sink. Where was Ted's sense of style? Shreds of broken glass bit into Evelyn's hand shredding her mind with distaste.

Never again. Never again. Evelyn in a house with no mirrors wandering restlessly around. Edging nervously up to a television screen, hoping it would give back her picture. Why did she feel so uneasy in a house with no mirrors? Was it vanity that could not be assuaged, or an insecure identity that needed to see a physical resemblance?

An air of menace pervaded the house that held no looking glass.

Glad to leave the house. Glad to leave the subtle dangers of her home for the safety of the courtroom. Safe in court. An orderly place. Her heart tidied up for the day's proceedings. Her steel will operating. "A woman of iron whim" Nick had once called her. Dry eyed as the jury filed in. Dry everywhere.

Then Nick, after three years abroad, re-entering her life. Striding through the door, in a bright cerise pink shirt, the button undone casually across the chest. Three years had been a long absence. Their hands reaching out. Nick's fingers still adorned by the two gold rings. Nick preening, wanting to show off in town, suggesting they changed for dinner, changing into a proud blue peacock, carefully choosing Evelyn's favourite shade of turquoise, an expensive pure silk shirt. Ready to leave, glancing this way and that, pleasuring Evelyn with such an exotic appearance, prancing this way and that, an amazing exotic bird, ready to take flight. Ready to take off. Take off that shirt, it is only a modest restaurant. No time. They had booked a table. Evelyn was never late.

"Where are the damn mirrors? A house without a single mirror! Isn't that carrying stringency too far?"

Later, the joint acquisition of the full length glass with the plain pine frame. Evelyn's choice. "Nothing ornate darling, please. We do have to live with it." As always placed carefully on Evelyn's charge account.

Watching Nick undress through the plain pine framed mirror. Nothing ornate. Happy to live with it. With the unadorned figure in the full length glass. Nick full length. Evelyn's acquisition. Your body is almost perfect, she breathed. Long, long torso, long, long legs. She did not, of course, say such a thing aloud. There was already enough evidence of the fullness of her love. So full she was frightened it might one day spill over. A messy thought. She shifted it away at once.

Would I love you just as much if you were scarred? Victim of an incurable disease? That might bring out the martyr in me. I am a good clean nurse. Highly efficient. But what would I feel about a bad case of dermatitis? What would I feel if two of those slender fingers were chopped off where the gold signet rings are, chopped off by the electric saw you bought to deal with the logs at the country cottage? Dermatitis would spoil your skin. Beauty is only skin deep. But it is your skin I draw my fingers over, your skin I feel beauty through, your skin I knew from before.

Measured emotions were the lawyer's stock in trade. Something intemperate about this love. This love could no longer be allowed.

"One day you'll come upon some emotion you can't file away in your boring grey metal Twinlock. You won't be able to live with that, so what will you do? Women like you are killers. You will kill it off! But first you will compartmentalise, rip it neatly apart, that done, you will kill it off."

She shuddered at the memory of the words. Ted's words? Nick's words? What did it matter?

Had she already killed it off? She was not known to be a killer. What have I killed in my time? Nothing advertently, but accidents will happen. Houseplants die whilst in my care. Unlike you, I do not have green fingers. Bodies die whilst in my care. Two of those slender green fingers chopped off where the gold signet rings are. Beauty is only skin deep but I draw my fingers over your skin. Over your putrid green skin, dead rancid flesh, drawn back by a lawyer's sensible stubby white fingers with their short clipped nails.

I am not known to be a killer but accidents will happen.

The borrowed car got bumped when I left it in a car park. You borrowed it because you had already bumped off mine. My car. My precious car. That car, a cause, a source of bitter contention. Insured in both their names. Paid for jointly. (Except when the running costs grew excessive.) Driven mainly by Nick. Permanently established in the public eye as Evelyn's car. Bumped off by you, you my darling, you who can always find another car to borrow.

The borrowed car left alive in the car park. No thought of killing anything, killing anyone. I am not known to be a killer. A careful woman. A considerate driver. I left it in a University car park. It should have been safe enough there. All the other drivers had to have permits, had to hold degrees, doubtless belonged to the University squash club, no ordinary car park. A very suitable place to park a lawyer's borrowed car. It should have been safe enough there.

How did the accident happen? Are there such things as accidents? Was it an accident that she and Nick were doing time together? You have more time to do than I, and I mind, Evelyn thought.

PART TWO

I mind, Evelyn thought. I mind that you are late again. I mind particularly that you are late for this particular lunch. She glanced down at her large gold wristwatch. Luminous green face. Bold figures. A cleverly contrived timepiece suitable for the surreptitious sneaky looks she shot at it in court. We are still doing time together and it is my time you waste. Are you even now spending my time changing your shirt? Will you slide in, tardy and unrepentant, a dilatory elegant pink flamingo, aloof and tall, lighting up this unpretentious restaurant with your pink and red plumage?

Why was Nick always unpunctual? This time, not yet inconsiderately late, but sufficient to make her own promptness an exasperating reproach. Sufficient to cut down the precise one hour and fifteen minutes she was sparing between court appearances.

She felt in her pocket and took out the two brown envelopes. In one was Nick's rent, in cash. Always the same amount. Always in crisp twenty pound notes. In the other there was a sum of money that varied from week to week. It was for fresh vegetables and fruit. With it this week she had attached some recipes which she had carefully cut out of a French magazine.

There was, she realised with annoyance, absolutely no

need for her to do this. Nick, unlike Ted, was a surprisingly good cook. Ted, as she irascibly recalled, had never risen above cardboard scrambled eggs. There was no necessity to provide menus in French or in any other language. As usual Evelyn was being over-organising, over-protective, attempting to control and contain those she loved. And how she did indeed love Nick. She stared at the menu and shivered at how vulnerable she felt.

Why did she behave like this? Why did she simply not pay the money into Nick's bank account? Why had she opened that account at her own branch? She began to flagellate herself, toying restlessly with the solid silver knife and fork as she did so. Perhaps after all Henri's did have pretensions.

In the borrowed minutes left to her, the woman who did not deal in commonplaces now resorted to dull and boring self-recrimination. A galaxy of banal reproach, a wealth of tedious castigation. Was this the state to which love led? If so, she would have no more of it. She was glad the decision had already been taken.

The truth was she enjoyed protecting and controlling Nick. The truth was she looked forward to meeting Nick in this restaurant and luxuriously lingering over a first class meal before they raced back together to the delights of the new slum. A description Nick had mockingly attached to the apartment she had fastidiously found and settled upon, which if not sumptuous could hardly be designated a hovel.

The truth was she was frightened that if she did not offer the rent and food money, Nick would abandon her. As Ted had abandoned her. She was too rigid, too analytic, too cold...no...not always cold, surely Nick knew that.

"You are a typical lawyer! Your mind is like a filing cabinet. Every thought in its appropriate pigeon hole. Neatly labelled. Competently categorised. What you love best in the world is meticulously tracing abstruse references and footnotes and indexing them first alphabetically by subject then alphabetically by author. If you could grade and seed love and affection, you would! If you could classify and catalogue despair and hate, you would! What you need is a standard size robot to take care of, not a relationship with a real human being!"

Which of them had stormed at her with those taunts? Some days the similarity in their strictures led her to confuse their demandingly different personalities. The fluent style of *those* sneers, the acid mockery concealing more than a grain of truth, led her to the miserable conclusion that it had been Nick. The argument had occurred after she had decided they could no longer live harmoniously together in the same house. During those first tempestuous months she was still keeping Nick. Still keeping Nick away.

"Why don't you ever let go?" Nick raged.

But they both kept coming back for more. Perhaps neither of us can fully let go, Evelyn thought.

You can't standardise emotion, you can't neaten up the passions like you try and do, you can't make them all fit into boxes! Some of them, some of us, spill over, and what will you do about that? Nick was trembling with crossness and excitement, the short spiky blonde hair pushed back, beads of perspiration standing out like raindrops.

"My love, my love, I am not going to do anything," she said slowly, her hands reaching for the exquisite face, relentless with rage, alight with frustration. She stroked the fair spikes of hair, trying to make her fingers reach where her words failed. Was their communication problem only one of unequal power relations? Without the age difference…to Evelyn, twenty-three years was a significant age difference… would Nick have been able to love her in the way she was beginning to need more acutely each day?

"I am not trying to box in you and your passions," she added, for the benefit of the record clerk in her mind, but they both knew she was lying. The substance of the charge was accurate. Nick's arrangement called her very soul to account. She used words like freedom and justice as a litany but she grew disturbed at the idea of a genuine liberation that allowed for emotions she could not herself keep under control. Margins and leeway she accepted, but anything bordering on excess she had learnt to dread. Liberty Hall was Evelyn's personal hell. She would go to extraordinary lengths, as Nick knew well, to stop anything spilling out over an edge. In court if she spotted a speck of dust, her impulse was to trap it at once. She would place her palm firmly over it, and ensure it could not roll out, could not spill over. There would be no dust on the Prosecuting Counsel's desk. All would be in order.

During the Disorderly Days she had tried painstakingly to imprint small patches of perfection upon their bedraggled domesticity. She would arrange Ted's tools in straight lines. She would allow no ink blots upon her own immaculately typed papers. If she baked a cake, a surprisingly frequent occurrence as she later recalled with shy surprise, she would first marshal the ingredients then rationalise them into a soldierly display by colour and texture. Irregularities dismayed her, she was a woman who craved perceptible boundaries with herself well within them. Even her role as wife, Ted Catullo's wife, did not upset her. It ensured she knew who she was, it offered her a fixed identity, an area in which she could safely repose, a cliff to rest against, high above the abyss.

Evelyn found a silver sureness in the constructed precision of their daytimes. Ted on the other hand revelled in the sensual abundance, the jungle brawls of their nights, for in the early years her desire to disinfect did not extend to their gloriously shambolic and frequently frowzy bed.

Later Ted's patience ran out. He began to hate the order she had ferociously imposed on their rackety existence. Hated the way she tidied him up, tidied away his possessions.

"Life isn't tidy any more than I am! Why can't you leave me alone, Evelyn, why can't you keep your damn files in order, but leave me free?"

Constant calumny. Vituperative attacks. Month after month, year after year, they increased in viciousness.

"For God's sake, Evelyn, stop straightening up the bloody house and straighten up the mess that's inside, for inside you are as dead and closed up as your musty old cases!"

The last indictment was delivered the night before Ted left with the odiously scruffy baby sitter, the girl with loose scraggly hair and, Evelyn thought sourly looking at the red love bites on her neck, morals to match. Obviously a unique and special baby sitter. The only one who failed to wash up properly, the only one who left grease marks in the sink.

"She is the only one for me. I am sorry Evelyn."

But he did not sound sorry. He sounded triumphant. Ted Catullo, reigning King of Disorder. About to descend into Hades without a Hoover.

"Daphne is so free-spirited, so hedonistically indulgent, she will just pee with pleasure when I touch her," Ted revealed proudly in the drunken row before he finally departed. Evelyn froze with repulsion. Was it possible that she had allowed intimacies, that she had allowed herself to have a child with a boor as lacking in taste and sensitivity as this?

Recently Nick's sloppiness had begun to remind her of Ted, of the old forgotten ways, the old suppressed resentment. Was it once more her tidy habits that had forced Nick to leave? But Nick had not left as Ted had left. Nick was pushed. (Push away that thought. Time for that thought later.) Time. It was certainly time Nick should have arrived.

She looked impatiently at her wristwatch then around the restaurant. Beige suede walls. White damask tablecloths and napkins. Fresh pink freesias on every table. Familiar, discreet, orderly and of course expensive. A restaurant they frequently lunched at. Evelyn's choice.

"Why do we not ever go anywhere simple so that I could have the pleasure of paying?" Nick would occasionally protest. Sometimes they did. But it would be Evelyn's money Nick paid with and neither of them would comment. Honour had been temporarily saved. Respect renewed. She did respect Nick. She respected the brains, the beauty, the blossoming dramatic flair. Nick was at drama college on a scholarship, training, determined to act more than well paid bit parts.

"You want to be a star my darling, don't you?" Evelyn would gently tease, in the tender calm that came after one of their red-hot rows.

"And you will be, I know that."

She did know that. Years of observation in the courts had made her a keen judge of character and ability. It would not be long before her love had flown and no longer needed her help. Why did that thought distress her so much? Why could she not allow anyone she loved to be their own person? Love is not about belongings.

Well, she had finally come to a decision. This time she would not wait to be deserted. She would push Nick away today. Before the pudding.

Henri's was less crowded than usual today. The last time she and Nick had lunched here, every table had been taken. A man dining with his wife and teenage son at an adjoining table had covertly watched them throughout two courses, monitoring their dialogue, growing attuned to the familiar way they responded to each other. Then he had leant across to his wife and said in one of those confidential tones that those seated several feet away cannot fail but hear: "See that pair...the age difference is so striking they could..."

The rest of the sentence was lost in the clatter of cutlery as the waiter attended them.

Nick and Evelyn had flashed each other an amused glance. Evelyn had held out her hand, and Nick had reached for it, clasping it too hard, clinging almost, saying "No, no, I'm not," as petulantly as might the teenage boy at the next table. They had both laughed and she had held on tightly to the hand, making a pinky red mark, darker than the trembling petals of the freesias. The mark on the hand or was it the flowers were left glowing burning in her mind this lunchtime, a different lunchtime, a different day, waiting for the same hand to slide across the table past the tall vase of fresh flowers with the same scent.

That day, after the laugh...one of those rare laughs that tug at the mind later...one of them had said comfortably: "With a relationship like ours, age does not matter." It does not matter which of them had said it. In a relationship like theirs the unspoken rules were known to both of them. And both of them knew when it was safe to speak them aloud.

"You get on so well together, considering the enormous difference in your ages," some of Evelyn's women friends would say enviously, wondering why it did not happen to them, surprised at their sudden impulse to stroke back, very gently, very softly, the wayward tufts of fair hair on Nick's striking bold head, Nick who suddenly did not seem so youthful.

"Having a loving relationship is not dependent on age,"

Evelyn would assert stoutly using Nick's phrase, one it had to be admitted she was a trifle tired of listening to. The phrase of the unfledged yearling. Used by one who has yet to find out that it may not be true. Evelyn using it with the wisdom and hope that occasionally comes with middle age, in the slightly scared voice of the woman in her middle years, who needs it to be true.

She recalled Nick's mocking tones, the provocative amendment: "Having a loving relationship is not dependent on anything. Not on age. Not on colour. Not on sex!"

The twinkle in Nick's blue eyes lit up a small fear quickly crushed in Evelyn's heart. Who else was Nick seeing? Did Nick tell her everything? Did Nick have lovers she did not know about? Were they women, older women, as old as she was? Could they be men? Why did it matter? Nick was right, such facts were no concern of hers.

She knew the lines. She felt the fears. She stifled the anger. She felt for the brown envelopes. She was the older woman in charge of the cheque book. She was the woman who had loved too long in the old ways, and was too old, too tired, to learn the new, or at least too battle fatigued to keep putting them into practice. For her the war was coming to an end in a restaurant with beige suede walls and fresh pink freesias on the tables. A warrior in a long black gown and cleverly tinted hair under the close fitting wig was retiring from battle. Before dessert. There would be no medals. No dubious decorations. Just absence and a long period of time to get over the pain. She was at home with time. It was her partner. She and time had used each other well.

She thought back, memory drifting like the pink petals in front of her, this last year had been the hardest. There were still scars from these last twelve months. Scars that would take more months to heal than she and Nick had left together.

The age difference had begun to seem greater than ever. Nick was beginning to want different things from those they had jointly planned. (Those she had planned and Nick had sunnily agreed to.) Nick wanted a worldwide acting career. Television. Stage. Films. All that was possible. Wanted to travel. Wanted to have adventures. (Evelyn had once wanted adventures, now it was peace she craved.) See India. Japan. Might even want children. (Or want someone who wanted them…) Though that was not mentioned often. Nor was the menopause. She had finished with having children. "And you never got much out of it, did you dear?" Nick scoffed. "Always too busy with your work to pay the right kind of attention!"

"How would you know?" she seethed under her breath. "What do you know about what it is like to have children? You are hardly more…"

Wisely she broke it off, did not say it aloud. Nick needed to break away, break it up. Nick knew which lines would break her down, break her. She would not retaliate.

After they had re-established peace and were toasting each other in pink champagne, Nick said fervently: "I want it all!"

Rose Epernay by Marguerite Christel, Nick's favourite. The pink liquid bubbling. Nick laughing at her above the bubbles.

"I do, I want it all."

The delicate curves of the champagne bottle. Cuvée de reserve. Dry. Life without Nick, what would it be like? She, put on one side. Dry. Dry everywhere. Once more wanting so little. And Nick now wanting it all. What could she say? She who had had so much of it, had seen India and had been slightly repelled, had visited Japan on a cultural embassy tour, and had been slightly bored. What right had a woman of fifty to respond by saying: "Darling, you cannot have it all. Life will stop you. It will deal you blows. You will go under like I have gone under."

Could she add, you will survive like I have survived? Was Nick the survivor that she herself had been? How could either of them assess that when the subject in question was a mere twenty-seven? At least Nick was not weak like Ted. It had to be admitted that somewhere uncomfortably tucked into her subconscious, she had a sneaking affection for weak dependent men. They did not challenge her control in the way Nick did.

Let me go on protecting you. Just for a little while. Let me go on helping, advising, guiding. OK leave the house, live somewhere else, leave me, leave the house that has been your home for so long...

"It has never been my home. Never. You talked about sharing it. But you don't know how to share. This place has always been yours. Paid for with your money. Decorated to your taste. Controlled by your decisions. Organised in your way. Even my studio was chosen by you, tidied up by the woman you pay an insignificant amount to work for you! I am just a visitor. That is what I have always been. A visitor in your house!"

Evelyn was appalled. "Darling you are not a visitor. You are...you are..." She searched for the most significant, the most meaningful term she could find, something that would move this dear irritating self-willed angry creature. She could have said "You are my love, my dear love," but she went on searching for some word that held more importance than lover or friend...

"Darling, you are....you are...you are my FAMILY."

It was the single worst word she could have picked upon. "Family!" Nick's voice rose to a shriek. "You would choose a word like that. A Capitalist Patriarchal noun! Families are traps. Homes are traps. There is no freedom in families or in the households run on nuclear family lines like this one. And there is beginning to be no freedom in this relationship. Love does not have to be stuck in a house, encased in some family-like set up to exist. It should exist between two free people or not at all. Homes and families and friends and lovers the way you invent them are traps. Love the way you use it is a trap. I feel trapped. By your money, by your love, by your damn damn power. Of course I find it attractive. Compelling. As I find you. Everyone I meet tells me you are the most interesting, the most remarkable woman they know, and how lucky I am. How can I dispute that? I who know, I who daily live with it. But it is ceasing to interest me. I cannot be compelled any longer by the nature of your particular compulsions."

Tall and bright with your anger you stand, towering above me, there are eleven inches between us...and now as many miles...the pent-up force of that terrible anger striking at me, gleaming like a polished axe. And I wanting to strike back. Wanting to strike you. Take up the axe. Use it. Use it. Remember how we used to swing the axe before we bought the electric saw for the logs at the country cottage? Remember how I taught you to swing it? Take off the signet rings, I'd say, you might catch them. Watch your fingers, I'd say, you might cut them. Chop them off, accidentally. Accidents will happen. Nick angry with her. Love does not have to be stuck in a house. Homes and families are traps. Nick's fingers, long slender fingers trapped by the two heavy gold signet rings. They had been a very special birthday present. Love the way you use it is a trap.

Why don't you ever let go? LET GO. Push Nick away. Push memory away.

Damn damn power. Damn you, damn you. Evelyn pushed the silver knife and fork away from her and near to sobbing put her head for a moment on the white damask tablecloth.

Quickly she wiped her eyes, recovered herself, then she looked up. There in the doorway of the restaurant, twenty minutes late, was Nick. A stunning six foot two inches of splendour, immediately the most striking person in the room. Flaunting a startling turquoise shirt, like some crazy brazen peacock, the fluorescent blue-green lit up against the pure white crushed silk jacket and trousers. A fluorescent sea blue-green marker in sea water the same colour, tossing against white silk furling waves. A blue bombarding radiation producing excited atoms at every table in Henri's.

In the trouser pocket, edging out roguishly was a matching turquoise silk handkerchief. The suit from Millbridge's most luxuriant gentlemen's outfitters had been so expensive that the manager had offered Nick the handkerchief free. The suit had been Evelyn's last present to her beloved. They had been invited to a Law Dinner at which Evelyn was to give an opening speech. "I want everyone to notice you, dearest," she had whispered proudly, murmuring to herself: "How could they not? How could they not?" Nick was hers. Her very own.

Stop it, she whispered. Stop it. Ownership has nothing to do with love. Love is not about belongings. You can lose both if you are not careful. This new relationship was bringing out the same destructive urges that her fifteen year old marriage to Ted had produced in her.

She watched Nick loll casually against the doorway then catch sight of her and begin to smile. Without wanting to she smiled back, watching closely the flaming blue beacon light up Henri's discreet cream and white restaurant.

Nick strode confidently down the length of the room to their table. Reached her chair and stood for a few seconds behind her. One hand stroked the back of her neck, the other was round her shoulders. She felt the long slender fingers stroking her. Stroking. Awkwardly.

For a moment she thought she felt the gold signet rings press into her flesh, then she remembered. A shudder ran through her shoulders. She shook the hand off. She touched the two brown envelopes and drew strength.

Nick was studying the menu. "I'm late. Forgive me. Have you ordered without me? I should not blame you." Nick caressing her with the words.

"Of course I haven't. Don't worry darling. There's nothing to forgive." Lying, caring, indulgent as always. Unable to be hard now that Nick was here. Maybe this was not the right moment, Evelyn thought. Wavering as she had so often done before. At least let us not spoil the pleasure of Henri's hors d'oeuvres. They were after all something quite special.

The waiter arrived and Nick nonchalantly ordered with habitual grace. What could she say that would make it easier for both of them? While her adroit mind went on planning her speech, she chatted pleasantly, telling Nick about the curious case she was involved in. Suddenly she realised her luncheon partner was no longer listening. Nick had stopped eating, pushed away the plate, and was leaning forward across the table, looking intently at her with a strange expression she had not seen before.

"There is something very important that I need to say to you. And I need to say it before you hand me over anything. It is something I have been wanting to say for a very long time…"

PART THREE

An elegantly dressed woman of about seventy-five wearing a beige linen suit edged with navy paused wearily for a moment in the doorway leading from the hall. She was still not used to the shuffling movement left by the stroke. With one faintly wrinkled hand she re-adjusted her spectacles. Their large navy blue rims gave her a somewhat severe look, enhanced by the coils of iron grey hair expensively coiffured and rigidly disciplined into two smart plaits on the top of her head. She drew in her breath and let a small sigh escape. Then tightening her hold on her stick, she tapped her way as briskly as she was able into a communal lounge. She knew that she was much better dressed than the other residents of the Windlesham Manor private home and this allowed her a stance more assured than her feelings.

Several of the elderly occupants had pulled their chairs into a semi-circle in front of the fire and were chatting under the tutelage of a rather plain woman in a plaid skirt and striped woollen shirt, both slightly shrunken but very noticeably of good quality.

"My son pays for me and never lets me forget it, and I am not alone in that particular predicament," the plain woman said portentously looking around her in a signif-icant manner.

"No, sadly, Miss Porter, you are not alone in that situation," said a much older man whose posture might once have been found in the army. "My own daughter is a very kind girl, and she and her husband foot the bill willingly and hardly ever grumble." He paused to reflect on the accuracy of his statement. Then natural cynicism or stern army training overtook him. "Duty! Damn sense of duty, that's all it is. My own daughter." He coughed and spluttered his rage and disappointment as he shuffled his way around a lounge he might once have strode through.

"Damn sense of self-preservation you mean, Colonel Stanley!" said the elegantly dressed old woman in the navy edged linen suit looking steadily out through the large navy rimmed spectacles, missing the Colonel's sharp eyes by a couple of inches. Her voice brittle with scorn.

"They will pay anything, do anything, as long as they do not have to have us living with them."

She tapped ferociously on the polished wood floor with her white stick.

It was the truth and everyone in the Residents Lounge of Windlesham Manor knew it. It was not a truth that the residents rested easy with. It became necessary now to turn on their tormentor.

"Well how about you, Duchess?" said the plain woman in the shrunken pure wool sweater. The vulgarisation at the end of the sentence did not come easily to the tightly buttoned lips of the former schoolteacher.

The elegant occupant with the white stick decided the jumper was probably cashmere. There were times when she had felt quite sorry for Miss Porter but this was not one of them.

"I should rather, Miss Porter, that you did not refer to me as Duchess," she said in her habitual proud ringing voice.

A voice once used to commanding attention. She turned to walk away from the others, turned too fast, not being able to see, anger shifting slightly askew her intimate knowledge of every corner of this cage. She lurched on the edge of a table, stumbled and fell losing her grip on the stick. Within seconds a nurse was by her side, helping her up.

At Windlesham Manor, help of a sort, smooth and white starched, was always at hand. For a price.

"Oh the Duchess always pays for herself. Hidden wealth from the past, eh Duchess?" said the Colonel, who had not yet finished with her.

"We have seen you handing over the correct money, in those neat brown packages. Little tips as well. Not much escapes our notice, my friend. Very organised of you, Duchess. Did they teach you to be that efficient at Law School?"

Before the old woman could gather strength and subdue fire enough to answer, the nurse intervened.

"It will be Guest Time in a few minutes, Ladies and Gentlemen. I want you all to go back to your rooms and have a little tidy up. Come along, Mrs Catullo. I shall be your good companion."

With that, she led the smartly dressed old woman out of the sitting room. Once outside in the hall, Evelyn Catullo allowed herself to lean heavily upon the nurse's protective arm.

Quarter of an hour later the Residents Lounge started to fill up with a bevy of nervous uncomfortable looking visitors who alternately attended to their aged relatives and to their modern quartz wristwatches.

Mrs Evelyn Catullo now attired in a bright red silk shirt stood white stick in hand at the side of the room. Waiting. She did not need her sight, she did not need her gold wristwatch, to know that her visitor would be late. Indeed already was. The statutory Visiting Hour was not even

that. By popular request it had recently been reduced to a
mere forty minutes. Fifteen of these had already struggled
by whilst the old woman stood upright and alone in the
Communal Lounge.

Once indomitable and fearless, finally in these last years
she had met fear and had given in. The accident followed
swiftly by the stroke had at first badly disabled her. But she
had fought back. As she had always fought. Determined to
regain a measure of her old control. Regaining her sight
however was beyond all skills. The numerous operations had
left her dogged with a kind of relentless patience which she
was now using. After a further five minutes had dragged by
and the already restrained conversations between Visitors and
Patients were becoming steadily more halting, the lounge
doors were thrown open. The vision of a tall imperious
looking visitor, with swinging fair cropped hair, possibly
middle aged but youthfully attired in a spectacular rainbow
coloured silk jacket with trousers, with matching rainbow
suede shoes, was offered to everyone in the room except the
object of the Visitation.

"Goodness me!" gasped Miss Porter to her well-bred
but hard pressed looking son, watching the rainbow suited
vision sweep across the room to the old woman with the
stick, give her a fast and affectionate hug, and taking hold
of her arm, march her trimly out of the crowded lounge
towards the empty dining room. As they passed the nurse,
the Visitor said persuasively in a deep bell like voice: "I know
Mrs Catullo prefers to be alone with me. It is alright if we
take up occupation in the dining room, is it not, Nurse?"

The deep bell tones were irresistible.

"Of course, of course it is," the nurse fluttered indulgently. "May I just say how wonderful I thought you were in that
last play, indeed how wonderful we all thought you were, you

know, the one that was televised, it had a big haystack in the first scene, you came proudly out from behind it. We all sat enthralled in the Lounge, well all of us except…"

"Of course Nurse, how very kind."

And the Visitor walked on firmly leading the navy spectacled old woman.

In the empty dining room they pulled up two hard chairs and sat opposite each other.

"Are they treating you alright?"

"Oh yes," said the old woman. "There is no need for you to worry. I have had some old legal cases done in Braille so that I may be able to get some of my interest back. The boredom is much worse than the pain. The daily dependence is much worse than the ongoing knowledge that I shall never see again. Never see the sunlight, although I can feel the evening warmth drift in through these windows."

She glanced accurately through the large spectacles in the direction of the open casements.

"Never again see the colours you are decking yourself out in, my darling, though I may by touch and memory be able to work it out."

She deftly ran her fingers up and down the rainbow silk jacket, then followed the line of the trousers and lingered there a minute, then she shivered and withdrew.

"I do not know," she said sadly. "It has been so long. I do not know what you are wearing today."

"I am sorry, Mother, it is something new, something I bought myself. It is rainbow coloured. Pure silk. Suede boots to match. I think you would approve."

"Nick, oh Nick, of course I would approve, I have always approved of you and your highly coloured flamboyant ways."

"It was sometimes hard to tell!" Nick said sharply, then looked aghast, and pushed the chair back. Ancient rows had not been on the Visitor's agenda, time was running out.

"Let us stick to business, Mother. I have brought the chocolates as usual, your favourites. Terry's 1767. Plain."

"And is the …?" the old woman broke off nervously, her hands for the first time straying from the stick, reaching for the Visitor's hands. They were not available.

"Of course. The brown envelope with the exact money for the Warden is in the bottom of the box. Beneath the second layer. It is the larger of the two envelopes. The small envelope contains four five pound notes for you to hand out to anyone who has been particularly good to you."

"Dear heart, it is you who have been particularly good to me. I am so very grateful."

Again she reached for the Visitor's hand and again found nothing. Stiffly she returned her own to the white stick and found if not comfort there at least familiarity.

Visiting Hour was almost up. The rainbow suited Visitor in common with all the other more quietly clad visitors had a green eyed luminous wristwatch.

"I shall have to fly, Mother. Rehearsals for the New York play start tonight. I must not be late."

"Is it going well? Will you be a success? I do so wish I could be there to see you perform." The old woman's voice was over-eager.

The Visitor had already risen, was already somewhere else. How do you retain a brilliant bird in flight?

"Darling Nick, may I ask you something? Why did you suddenly decide to change your name? You were becoming so well known as Nick Catullo. Your father would have been proud."

"Mother it is YOU I wanted to be proud."

The voice rose in exasperation and despair. "I wanted something from you, Mother. The only thing that you did

not give me, that I could finally take, that you no longer
needed, could no longer use, was your name. When you
had the accident and then that terrible stroke, when you
could no longer practise, when you no longer needed to
be the great Nicola Evelyn, I could finally stop being your
baby Nick. I could be my own person, Nicola, and borrow
the name of Evelyn from you. I could be Nicola Evelyn."

The tall woman in the startling rainbow coloured silk
suit bent down and hastily handed across the chocolates,
forgetting in her haste to transfer them to the other hand.
The clumsiness of the gesture, the fumbling of the fingers
did not match up to the poise and glamour of the colour
co-ordinated outfit.

Without touching the older woman she walked swiftly
out of the room.

OCTOBER PHOTOGRAPH

I n my flat overlooking the cold Cornish beach, I see scudding shivering children dredging up polished British pebbles, smooth and shiny, silver washed. The children plump them into piles on the sludged sand or drip them back into the navy sea, ruffling the chill surface.

On my dull cream bedroom wall...the dull creaminess, the cream dullness, a product of poor paint and poor ideas ...is blu-tacked your brown body, eight inches by ten inches.

Did I get my ruler out to chop your beauty into exactly measured segments? Order is critical to my evaluations so yes, perhaps I did.

In the photograph, blown up eight by ten, you too are on a beach, Emily, a hot stifling Greek beach, yesterday's sand, a summer's sand, white beneath the black shadow under your two white hands.

It is a poor print, a lying print, a false photo, your hands were brown (sweat dripped from them) photographed brown by my tanned hands. Yes we were baked to a tan, tan, in our pock-marked culture, ringing better than brown.

Your fingers (white lying fingers) press together, palms uppermost, cupping a batch of grey, white and pink pebbles.

(The pebbles steam.) Emily, you said firmly there were no black pebbles on a Greek beach.

In the photograph, in the background, hazy, behind your dark almost olive bare arm, (the arm that ended in the white hand) lazy, as it scratched the sand, (the sand steams) there are dozens more grey, white and pink pebbles, but look, yes, black pebbles.

It is a poor print, a lying print, a false photo. Or else you lied then as we lay together trying to tell the truth to each other.

On that last day, on that last beach, (we always had a choice of two, the still that matched your own repose, or the windy which I more often chose) you gathered stones, none of them black. You were fierce about that. I took photographs of you gathering stones, many of them now ripened and hardened (cooled off would you say?) in my darkroom into the false blackness.

There are brown indentations in whiteness, in the sand, where your steaming body had pressed, breasts uncovered.

I run my October fingers over your August gloss, press them hard into what looks like softness using the camera's sharp misleading eye as a guide.

In the photograph, your elbows which at that time had dug into the white sand appear to dig into the core of the black shadow beneath your quiet hands. (Later you dug your fingers into my core, as I lay beneath hands no longer quiet but wild. It was too hot in the hotel bedroom to photograph that.)

In the eight by ten, you are looking only at the pebbles. You have had enough of looking at the camera. Shall I one day have had enough of looking at you through the lens as you sift stones to mask the handling of the grey, white and racing pink thoughts.

If I could photograph those thoughts, should I get those wrong too? Would racing pink come out black?

CAFE MEMORIAL

T he plane is crowded. No empty seats. Despite the air conditioning I am alternately hot and cold, shivering and sweating, as if I have a fever. According to the brisk voice of the pilot, we are only fifteen minutes away from Rhodes airport.

Already I feel the Greek heat rise in the dusty air. I smell the profusion of roses that grow abundantly by the road side. The man sitting next to me is reading his guide book. With the familiar camaraderie of strangers who are never likely to meet again, he turns to me.

"I guess you know the ancient myth that says the sun god Helios fell in love with the nymph Rhodon and named the island after her? Great guy don't you think? Good place to fall in love eh?"

He laughs in an easy man to man fashion.

Pedantically I suggest that the word 'rhodon' probably meant 'rose'.

"Scholar eh?" He is not deterred.

To myself I acknowledge that the island is a good place to fall in love. As good as any.

I look again at the brief scribbled note I am clutching.

There are drops of moisture on it. My hand is sweating. There are a few drops on my trousers where my hand has rubbed the material. Meticulously I dab at them with a starched white handkerchief.

"Meet you in the Deja Vue"

That is all it says. Followed by the suggested date and time.

Black italic handwriting, slightly sloping. The jolt when I saw it on the hall mat. One forgets words but handwriting seldom. I had remained in the same Victorian house in North London for the last ten years so the letter found me without difficulty.

Will you be there? Will you be at the same table? Perhaps they have moved the tables around, changed the appearance of the restaurant that looks out on a garden of olive trees fronting the quiet street. I know the restaurant is still there. Punctiliously I had made an international call from England just to check. Had you made a similar call from the States? Somehow I doubted it. It was not your way.

After ten years will you look any different? Will you wear purple? I think of the lavender voile dress, falling in folds, on the cane chair, in the Deja Vue, which you wore at our last meeting.

We had grown fond of several Greek restaurants that season but the Deja Vue, for some reason, had amused you. Was it because the fervently loquacious Greek patron enjoyed the nightly exercise of your Americanised Greek? Or was it because he let his discreet British wife do most of the traditional Greek cooking?

Amidst the dzadziki, avgolemono and dolmades, my preferences, and those cheese filled tiropitas to which you were addicted, she served up a superb vegetarian English breakfast to tourists at any time of day. Frequently we ate Greek specialities, at lunch time, on the beach, then fell into our favoured seats at night for a late evening breakfast.

"Where else can you do that?" you had said. "Only in Rhodes! It is quaint! It is British and Greek and quaint and I love it."

For that remark you employed your cartoon American accent which you used when you were mocking. Curiously, the rest of the time, your voice was accentless. Born in Baltimore, world travelled, you nevertheless remained a person from nowhere. A woman weighed down by possessions but belonging nowhere, belonging to no-one.

My chattering travel companion, a more obvious American, is reading aloud again.

"In Rhodes, the past is all around you. Ancient Greek remains often come to light when a cellar is dug up." He pauses before adding the inevitable "Isn't that quaint?"

Do all cartoon Americans have only one adjective at their disposal? Emily, too, had called me a scholar as if it was less a profession than a problem.

"You would like to dig me up if you could, find out where I came from, discover what makes me collect beautiful objects. Unearth the reasons why I can't let anything go."

Any room you inhabited became a backdrop to a series of rainbow coloured collector's items. A careful hoarding of precious pieces. Precious to you. As you were to me.

Correction. As you *are* to me. As you have been for the decade of your disappearance.

The past is all around me. The day we had thought of sailing for Simi, the small island off the coast of Rhodes.

"We can bring back sponges," I had enticed.

You were busy, however, increasing your collection. That day, you had collected one carved and jointed wooden fish, threaded with gold, swinging on a blue rope, one pink and blue embossed pottery bowl scrolled with the Greek key symbol, and one six foot by twenty-six foot ornate rug with the same motif.

"How are we going to get that home?" I had protested. "*We* are not going to have to get it home. *I* am. Remember? Two different planes, two different cities!"

Two different time zones. There would be three thousand miles between us after months of closeness in which I had studied your behaviour as you wandered in and out of antique shops and gold bazaars, entering empty handed, coming out with your blue and purple striped Grecian bag stuffed full.

"Is it about ownership?" I had ventured.

"No!" You were firm and said no more.

Ownership. The legal right of possession. For you it had been something else. To come into your own. To hold your own. Ultimately to be on your own. Single and self-possessed but with your beauties gathered around you. On just one occasion, kneeling by a rock pool, in a lilac swimsuit with a green dragon embellished on it, you had used the verb. Or rather its past passive tense.

"I can't be owned," you had said quietly.

I had been asking you too many questions, trying to place you, attempting to pressure you into one of my orderly schemes.

"Don't try. If you try, I shan't resist but I shall simply disappear inside myself. You will find me gone."

"Do you know the city?" the American in the adjoining seat is talking again. "I've done London pretty thoroughly and I'd like to do the best of Rhodes sharpish. Know any good tavernas? Bit of bouzouki, local colour, know what I mean?"

Immersed in his guide book he hardly notices my lack of response. The plane is jolting, a slight spluttering sound from the engine. A few more minutes, then the airport bus then a long slow walk to refresh my memories. I had, as always, given myself plenty of time to stroll through the Knights' Quarter, pause momentarily by the moat, allow for a few minutes in the Turkish Quarter, allot time for a brief wander through Perikleous and Pithagora which enclose the Jewish area.

"Digging for your roots?" you had teased, the first time we had walked there.

The overcrowded plane journey now behind me, I leave the Old Town, and put on speed through the New Town until I reach the Astron on Kazouli Street. A small forty-two bedroomed hotel within easy walking distance of beach and town, the original brochure had said. But for the first five days we had occupied bedroom forty-one and had only moved out of it when hunger or fresh air became a secondary critical need.

Later I dragged you to see the marble head of Helios, the third century statue of Aphrodite and the Mycenaean vases in the Archaeological Museum. Then I allowed myself to be led away to the treasures you really wanted to see, the stones on the beach and the jewels in the bazaars.

Will you still look the same? Long pinkish hair, redder in the sun, that should have clashed with the colours you wore but never did. The hair that entangled the dangling earrings, exotic gold and garnet or gold and amethyst (another mismatch with the hair). I recall your resolute refusal to remove either earrings or bangles which had remained steadfast during the long period I knew you.

"I shan't budge on that one! Don't try and pressure me."

I reflect on the differences in my own appearance. Of course I am older. I must look older. They say men age better than women but I do not know if that is accurate. Assuredly, success, which I did not have when we spent that summer in Rhodes, breeds a certain smartness. Having moved from the status of pedagogue to that of moderately best-selling author, my style has subtly changed. I no longer wear my old white blazer over garish tee shirts and the white knee length shorts. Television appearances (the writer as performer, the don made accessible) now merit elegant white suits, and pastel silk shirts. You would approve of my cuff links. Thirty-six carat gold with a small blue sapphire set in each one.

Memories have softened me to a standstill. I am not a person who lingers. It is not in my nature. It had become one of the conflicts between us.

"Let's do it!" I used to say. Impetuous. Impatient. Impulsive.

"I am still thinking about it. Mulling it over," you would reply.

How different in character and in style we were. I with my need to plan, to organise, to look ahead, to hurry along. Emily with her desire to hang on, hang about, a desire which turned her talent for indecisiveness into a philosophical way of being. She moved all the time but gradually and slowly as if time had only the meaning she set upon it that hour.

Today, however, I have allowed myself a great deal of time. I could linger if I knew how. Unless Emily has transformed herself I doubt that she will be early for our appointment, even though it is one she has fixed herself.

I remember the strange occasion when we decided to visit a gypsy who told fortunes. Well, you decided. You saw the notice: "British visitors particularly encouraged."

"She will make you feel at home," Emily had said.

The gypsy assured us that she had two Greek aunties but her voice was decidedly east London. She had pressed into our palms, gazed into her crystal ball and spun her stories.

Most of it was make-believe and erratic but neither of us cared. One thing however she got absolutely correct.

To me she said: "Time is your essence, my British friend. You are always ahead of it, even obsessed by it."

I had laughed and admitted the veracity of her statement. Then she turned an affectionate look upon Emily.

"And you, my dear dreamer, to you, time will always lie in wait. To be late is not a problem. You are too busy with your fantasies to notice the here and now. If you are not careful you may be late for your own funeral!"

"I shan't let her!" I had protested. "I'll be there to hurry her along."

We had walked away from the gypsy's tent, amused by her, enthralled with each other, Emily's hair glinting in the warm reddish light.

That was the day you lost your suntan oil.

I remembered us searching frantically for it. Falling into the hot sand in our restaurant robes. The purple and the white striping the beige beach.

"We can't search properly for suntan oil, we can't scrabble in the sand....not in these clothes," you had said, half laughing at yourself (or at me), half genuinely frustrated.

"Let's strip then!"

We stripped down to our pants, unable to keep our hands off each other's bodies. You were the one who peeled away our pants while I fleetingly wondered if anyone else would chance this way looking for something they too might have lost. Their youth? Their craziness? Their tanning gel? The sand began to cool as we clung and stroked and loved until suddenly you interrupted our fever with a triumphant cry.

"There it is! There's the lotion!"

There it was, half buried in the sand beside us. Our wild movements had dislodged it.

I laugh wryly as I recall your excitement. Another possession regained. Your world put back in order.

I screw up my eyes so that I can see you standing naked, the purple folds of voile on the ground, holding aloft the gritty bottle of lotion.

"We mustn't let it go to waste!" you had said, streaking it over your small firm breasts. I can see the oil glisten on the edges of your tapering white nails.

We were late returning to the Deja Vue that evening but our table had been saved. We walked towards it holding hands.

"If we sit at the same side of the table we don't have to let go," you had said.

I look at my wristwatch. It is time to make my way towards 28th October Street. I make a small detour around by Mandriki harbour. Signs show there are sailings every morning for Simi, the heart of the sponge fishing industry, and the monastery at Panormitis, only an hour's trip from Rhodes. Perhaps tomorrow we could take that trip, the one we had talked of, and return with our sponges, like ordinary tourists. I feel a lift of pleasure at the mere possibility.

The man selling wooden puzzle fishes still has his stall by the quayside. Or perhaps it isn't the same man, maybe a son or a brother or cousin.

Halfway down 28th October Street stands the ornate wrought iron mansion that is No 72. On the railings that lead into the olive fronted garden, swinging in the slight breeze is the small black and white sign: "Deju Vue Restaurant: English Breakfasts Served".

I am home.

Inside, the flower clock on the wall reassures me that I am not late for our rendezvous. The cane chairs have been renewed, but the photos of the harbour drawn by the local artist we had spent time talking to are in their familiar places around the walls. Do the waitresses still earn the Greek equivalent of £9 a day? I am too shy to talk to the girl who leads me to our table with the reserved sign on it. It had always been you who chatted to the restaurant staff.

I order an ouzo and water and I settle down to wait.

Ten minutes pass. Nobody enters. Then twenty minutes, then thirty-five. I order a second ouzo and try not to feel agitated.

Finally the door swings open. A tall athletic looking man, with the kind of bronzed face that sporty Americans acquire playing tennis in the hot sun, walks confidently into the restaurant. He looks around, sees no-one he knows, and his steps falter. A slight air of nervousness mists his countenance. He looks anxiously first at his wristwatch then at the flower clock on the restaurant wall. He gazes intently at the occupants of all the tables nearest to him.

I had never seen him before, nor had I seen his photo, but I know who he is. For a moment I look at him intently, willing his discomfiture, then I half raise my hand in a mock salute.

All confidence gone, he walks over to me. I motion to him to draw up a chair.

"She wanted us both to meet here," he says. "I suppose it was a place that had some significance for her?"

"Some, yes," I say curtly.

He fumbles in his brown leather wallet. He takes out a photo. It is slightly faded. Even before he hands it over I know which one it is. Would we look absurdly young? Would our expressions look passé? Ten years shows up on photographs. Does love have a sell-by date on celluloid?

"She told me a waiter took it at your last meeting... well...er...I don't have to tell you that..."

He scurries his words in nervous embarrassment.

Without looking at me, still gazing at the photo, he says as if to himself: "Emily is wearing a purple dress. I never saw her in a purple dress. I thought I knew all her clothes. How funny that she had a purple dress."

He tails off and I wait.

"And you…you are in something white. The only thing she ever told me about you, apart from the fact that you are a professor turned writer, is that you often wore white. I once went into a book shop and looked at your photo on the book jacket. You were wearing white."

His nerves have disappeared. Now his voice sounds smug as if owning that single piece of information means he owns a small part of me. I feel weary of him. How long do the two of us have to wait for her appearance?

Why had she told him that one white fact? Why tell him anything? Or, for that matter, why not tell him everything? She had after all never told me anything about him except his name.

"It's a very Christian name," she had said with a laugh. "Stephen. A very Christian man. Kind in a firm Christian way. Born on Christmas Eve wouldn't you know? I expect when in the womb, he instructed his mother to get it right!"

Suddenly I remembered her dropping a second piece of information. Unexpectedly. Unable to retrieve it after she had let it go.

We had been idling an hour away in the Old City, lurking in leather shops and jewellers, she to touch the goods possessively, me to watch her taking possession. I had offered to buy her a small brown leather wallet.

"Oh no! Not a neat brown leather wallet. That's what Stephen has. Although he is usually a highly self-assured man, if he suddenly feels nervous in some alien's presence, he will pull out this neat little wallet. Then he will meticulously take out all the dollar bills, fold them carefully, put them in a small pile, count them, then press them into a tiny pleat and put them back in his wallet. I doubt if he even knows he is doing it. I cannot bear to watch him!"

Stephen gives me the photograph of you in the purple dress. He watches me closely waiting for some response. I take it without glancing at it, and put it in my folder, then I gaze at him indifferently. He starts to say something, coughs, then reaches out for his wallet again. From its brown interior he pulls out a pile of dollar bills. He puts them carefully on the small table between us, by the side of my cooling coffee. Then with a swift almost petulant gesture he folds them into a tiny pleat and puts them back into his wallet.

I want to laugh, or tell him he has forgotten to count them. Now both of us can feel smug.

"Is she with you?" I ask finally. I had not realised they would come together.

"Yes, she is in the car."

"Let's go outside and join her," I say.

I pay the check and we walk together through the olive trees in the front garden of the Deja Vue. I thought of the firm black olives we had eaten every day on the beach that summer. They no longer taste the same when you leave the sun and buy them from the supermarket.

He has parked his vehicle at the bottom of 28th October Street at the junction where the area sharply divides, rough and noisy one way, quiet and languid the other. Half a dozen small tough Greek boys are crowding round the bonnet. Two more are pelting the door with tiny pebbles. A flashy American car is seldom seen in this part of town. I stand back, a long way behind the gang, too far away to see inside the car, sweltering in the heat, wondering whether what is running down my cheeks is sweat or tears.

Stephen unlocks the car and makes some pathetic shooing gestures towards the boys, who laugh and keep flailing the pebbles.

I walk a few yards down the road, away from the car. Let him tell her I am here. A few seconds later he emerges from inside the car, holding a small Greek urn.

He walks slowly towards me.

"In her Will, she said she wanted you to sprinkle her ashes in a place only you and she had spent time in. She said you would know what to do." He gabbles his words.

More awkwardly than in his dealings with the photograph, he deals out the urn.

I take it and I cannot speak.

Without saying goodbye I walk away from him, moving steadily down 28th October Street. I do not turn until I reach the small church near the corner. Then fleetingly I look back. His shoulders are shaking. Perhaps he is sobbing. Or laughing. He straightens up, and I can just see that on the bonnet of the car lies his neat brown leather wallet. He is pulling out the pile of dollars bills, and with the now irritatingly familiar gesture of petulance he refolds them into a pleat.

I hold the Greek urn with the same care I had last held you and walk slowly through the town to the place on the beach where you had lost your sun tan lotion.

I walk now to what I judge to be the place, the burial site of the sun tan oil, caressing the urn as I move nearer. It takes a few seconds to recreate the small dented pit. A sharp wind has blown up and is urging the pebbles to frisk. I want to scatter your ashes into the hole but I know the wind, now fiercer, will lift and blow them across the beach. I cannot do it.

Irrationally I think how you would hate to see your ashes flying in all directions. You could never bear to let go of anything you had once owned or cared for. You could not bring yourself to give your old clothes to charity, so unused, unworn, they piled up on chairs, on sofas, they hung limply from hat stands, hooks and hangers. You could not bear to burn your ancient files or answered letters. They clung to desk tops, they perched on stools, they littered the piano. You had a hard job throwing out mouldy cheese.

"Oh not that tiny square of Camembert!" you would say with anguish or was it compassion?

No, scattering your ashes wildly to the winds would not be acceptable.

Wherever you went in the world, you took possession, and whenever you left you took something away with you. I suddenly remember that after our last supper at the Deja Vue you insisted we ran down to our special part of the beach. Not the tidy sandy part but the jagged area alive with rocks and stones, where multicolour pebbles were washed constantly in the waves.

"I have to collect something," you had said. "We need to go back to the Astron first and get the old red rucksack. Come to the beach and help me. Well, you don't need to help, just sit and talk."

What were you up to?

We were due to leave, you for the States, I for England, the next morning. Our cases were almost packed. We had between us scarcely a corner left in any of the bags. The only container still empty was the old red rucksack, *my* rucksack, which it appeared you now needed.

I watched in amazement as you walked from the edge of the sand into the water, backwards and forwards, collecting objects, small pebbles, large stones, hefty sized rocks.

You sifted and sorted them by shape and colour.

"The pink are lovely, rose pink, just like a Greek sunset, I'll stack those first. Then the grey…more like silver than grey, so many silver droplets. There are hardly any black pebbles though. Have you noticed that?"

An hour or so later you were piling them into the red rucksack.

"I can't just leave our beach. I need some of it to remember us by."

I thought you were crazy. So I tried to rationalise heaving a rucksack full of stones to the airport by suggesting that we built a Greek island rock garden when we set up home together. You just smiled at me.

Did you build it? Did you sit by your stones? I never knew. There never was a home or a rock garden. After the days on the beach and the evenings at the Deja Vue, after lugging the stones to the airport, I never saw you again.

You kept tight hold of everything you cared for except for us.

How ironic, I used to think, after all my efforts to make contact with you had failed, how ironic, that you should finally let go of something that might have lasted, that might have been of use.

But of course, as usual I am wrong. You were never less than unpredictable. You had not let go at all. You have been lying in wait. To you ten years is hardly more than a pause for dreams. Ten years' silence, then your letter. Ten years' absence followed by your seductive invitation.

"Meet you in the Deja Vue"

After ten years that was all it said. A single sentence followed by the suggested date and time. Black italic handwriting, slightly sloping. Ten years then the return trip to Rhodes. Ten years and now the Greek urn.

The urn with your ashes.

I move from the sandy beach over to the part that is shingle and stones. Here we are, I say to you, here we are, treading the same stones. This is the place.

Unlike you I do not know how to linger.

Suddenly, swiftly, I scatter you.

I scatter every last ash. There you are safely at home on your stones.

Then from nowhere the wind races, gets up speed, begins to tug at the ashes. They will move inexorably towards the sea.

Quickly I kneel. Efficiently I start to pick up the stones. First the pink ones, the rose glow of a Greek sunset, then the grey ones, grey like silver droplets, then the black shiny ones. You are right there are very few black shiny pebbles.

I put them one by one…each stone with some ashes clinging to it…into the new red rucksack.

"No, the rucksack wasn't expensive," I tell you. I know that in your careful caring way you will ask. "Just a hard wearing economical rucksack that a person needs. You can only wait a few years for a friend to return a bag then you have to purchase another."

I have no other bag with me. In the last ten years I have been travelling light.

The stones are heavy.

I wonder if the airline officials will put them in the hold.

SNOWSTORM

The wind swirled round us so that the snow stung our faces. I turned my back for a moment. I knew she was still there lagging a few steps behind, her thick-soled lace-up boots making a convivial crunch in the snow. It was the only companionable sound. She had dropped my hand after I had finally broken the silence and given her the news. I have never known how to deliver bad news gracefully. This time I was blunter than I had intended.

I had taken off and placed on a rock my thick red fleecy gloves in an attempt to warm one of Cressida's small hands between both of mine. She drew away. I had made no difference. Possibly I never had.

I snuggled one of my own chilly hands into my coat pocket and felt for the worn leather bookmark. It was a warm creamy colour decorated with violets and olive leaves. 'To Mother on Mothering Sunday' it read. Then the standard verse which thanked the heavenly Father for our parents 'especially our mother'.

Cressida had given it to me the spring before I had left. For the first year I moved it from book to book until it was too frayed to be a useful reading adjunct. Then I had placed it carefully in my desk drawer. Rarely sentimental I wondered why today I had put it in my pocket.

I stooped down and retrieved my ripe red gloves fluttering in the wind like scarlet butterflies on the grizzled rock. Snowflakes petalled the fingers.

Cressida was but a footfall behind me huddled inside her dull green jacket with two buttons missing. It was the same dreary jacket she had dragged on the last time I had seen her. Was it two years ago? Was it three? Aggressively I had told Charles to buy her a new jacket, something vivid.

"She doesn't like bright colours. She doesn't like bright lights. She isn't you," he had said courteously but with a certain satisfaction.

There are all kinds of lines which you would want to remember as the last words someone said to you ... even someone you did not much like ... however "She doesn't like bright lights. She isn't you" will not rank among my favourite memories.

Suddenly Cressida overtook me and raced ahead kicking up spurts of snow. We were quite alone in the hills. It was not yet dusk. I had brought her here so that we might exhaust ourselves with walking after I had told her the news.

In the early days ...was it nine years ago, was it ten? ... Charles had brought her here for picnics. He had always made her white bread sandwiches spread with peanut butter. On one visit I had accompanied them on the picnic.

"Have you ever tried salami or tomatoes with olive pâté on brown?" I had suggested.

"No we haven't," Charles had said politely. "Would you like that, Cressida?"

"No I wouldn't like that! We always have peanut butter. I LIKE peanut butter!"

The snowstorm was gathering strength. Cressida was

almost out of sight. I became anxious I would lose her again.

Several yards ahead of me, the dull green jacket flapped around her tense thin frame. A brittle green stick that might snap at the touch. What colour was her jumper underneath the jacket? Surely, I thought, I should be wondering if the jacket was sufficiently warm, as I hurried after the disappearing figure. Am I always trivial in the face of crisis?

I thought of Charles, the outrageously tall, immensely strong rock climber. I thought of Charles the healthy risk-taking mountaineer, the most courageous man I had known. How petty of Charles to die running for a bus. How petty of me to mind.

Did Cressida care how he died? She had said nothing, nothing at all, when I gave her the news. She just looked at me with dark green-grey eyes that reflected and outshone my own. Slowly she undid the four remaining buttons on her jacket. Then with treacherous precision she refastened them. I felt profoundly irritated. I was reporting her father's death and she was inadequately dressed for the announcement.

A harsh noise broke through the hillside. Branches were cracking and breaking. Cressida put her two hands, fingers splayed, round her neck as if to choke off further sounds. Then, her voice icily polite, she said: "Thank you, Kay. Thank you for coming all this way to tell me. Your usual style is letters."

From the day I told her I was leaving she had always called me Kay as a measure of disassociation from any relationship we might have had.

She was correct. I did write letters every week between writing articles for the fashion magazine which Cressida despised and which Charles tolerated with the amused compassion with which he tolerated all my English eccentricities. Cressida of course never answered.

Not once in nine years. I think it was nine, perhaps it was ten. Charles sent short courteous replies from outposts in Scotland inquiring politely about my vivid life. Vivid was their favourite term of vituperation.

"I wasn't vivid enough to accompany you was I, Kay? Not vivid enough to take along. I didn't match your outfits. I wasn't sufficiently smart or sufficiently stylish to fit into your leather briefcase."

Her hair that month had hung long and straggly obscuring the fine lines of her face. Sulky hair. Sullen hair that never looked quite washed. The mopish beige jumper that month had been stained or perhaps the washing machine had rejected it.

"I wore dowdy rucksacks with untidy straps. You saw me as bulky and unbecoming. I never became you. You could not wear me like a flower in your lapel, Kay. I had Fair Isle sweaters because Dad's mother, who understood me, knitted them. I remember once you said how common the Fair Isle stitch was. You meant it wasn't on the pages of Vogue. Charles will tell you it is very common here! We all wear it. Because this is Scotland and it's cold and we wrap up."

Charles would no longer be able to tell either of us what was currently the fashion in Scotland. Cressida's source of information had dried up. Her guide, her mentor, her dear love was gone. As I told her the news I put my arm out to shelter her. With a terrible fierceness she pulled away and started printing slow strangled footsteps on the path. It was Charles who had given her shelter for ten or was it only nine years? Protection was his style. Evasion and absence was mine.

How ridiculous for such a tall imposing man, six feet five inches in those ugly Fair Isle patterned socks, to die in a road accident. They told me on the phone that he had run for a moving bus, the number 102, jumped, slipped, fell on the road, and a lorry unable to slow down ran over and killed him.

Death was instantaneous they said. It always is. News of death I mean, the shock of death I mean, to the listener who hears it. I died his death on the telephone instantaneously. I suspect Cressida died his death on the cold hill path when I broke it to her. Instantaneously. 'Broke it to her.' What a stupid phrase. A phrase without a meaning. 'Broke her.' Now that's a phrase with meaning. Of all the people to break her inevitably it had to be me.

Cressida has stopped walking, allowing me momentarily to catch up. Alongside I sneaked a gaze to see if she had been crying.

"I haven't!" she said sarcastically. Charles had been psychic too. "I haven't," she repeated. "You ought to remember, Kay, that crying is something Dad and I feel is wasted emotion."

"Felt!" I wanted to correct her. "Felt not feel!" But I said nothing. What a clumsy death. How menial to die under a bus. Cressida shot me a long hard look. I felt the cold wind sweep over me. Snow was falling harder now.

"Why wasn't it you? Why did it have to be Charles? Why my father?"

I do not know if she said those words. But I heard them anyway. The words she spoke and the words she did not speak. Cressida never spoke much to me so today was no different.

"I thought we would walk for a bit longer if you are OK," I said.

"I'm OK. I would rather climb. You can wait or you can go. I am going to climb."

"Of course I won't go!" How tedious I sounded. She cast a despairing look at my bright new brogues. "I shall climb."

"Suit yourself," she said.

Six years ago, one summer, when I visited regularly, the

three of us had taken their favourite walk by the river. Charles had decided to hike off on his own for a couple of hours. Cressida and I were left to do the best we could. I had the train timetable in my pocket as a safety valve. I could always make an excuse and catch an earlier train.

We walked on as always in silence. I wondered why Cressida had not hiked up the hill with her father. Perhaps before I arrived he had asked her, gently but firmly, to let him go off by himself. Or perhaps they had agreed that I should be allowed two hours with Cressida for my request. To plead my case as Charles detachedly put it.

Cressida and I had reached the river. The sun glowed on the water. A mottled toad gurgled. We sat divided by her shabby green rucksack. There were dismal badges of hostels she had visited pinned on one of the straps. I expect she was proud of the number of youth hostels she had hiked to. She gave a look of disdain at my new pale and white striped linen daysack. In silence we lay by the river. Her breathing seemed hushed. I was the first to break the quietude.

"I know what I want," I said tentatively.

"I know what IS!" she said fiercely. "Charles and I live here together. No matter what you want NOW you can't change that! It doesn't matter what you want now."

"I want, I would like, I need more time with you. Down south. Where I have an apartment. Perhaps a few weeks in your vacation."

I broke off, jagged, incompetent.

In the stifled voice of someone reading aloud from a foreign phrase book she said: "Flat! You have a FLAT. Not an apartment. Holidays! I have HOLIDAYS not vacations!"

"It's living abroad." I felt nervous. "Travelling. The States. Apartments, vacations, closets, subways. Coming back it's hard to remember, hard to get it right."

She had stopped listening to me. Instead she was mouth-
ing words into her reflection caught by the sun in the river.

"He needs me. You were the one, Kay, who told me that."

I had been the one who told her that. "Your father needs
you, Cressida, more than I do. He needs you to stay with
him." My escape clause. Or the shutting of the trap door.

Had I said it to her? Is that where she heard the phrase?
Perhaps she heard it from the others. Family, friends, those
without families of their own, those without friends. All
horrified and shocked. Mothers, good mothers that is,
hardly ever run away.

Certainly it was a phrase she had picked up years ago like
those first sentences in the foreign phrase book. Pass the
marmalade. The hospital is on the left. Where is the railway
station? She had not been given a translation. When you
learn a foreign language those first crucial sentences stay
with you the longest. Pass the marmalade. He needs you.
The hospital is on the left. Your father needs you. Where is
the railway station? He needs you more than I do. Those
are the phrases you hear and rehear, those are the phrases
that become your sentence.

Abruptly Cressida had leapt from the river bank, then
had swiftly run across the grassy patch. I watched her long
legs. I watched the sun dappling them. Gold brown spots
on long tanned legs. She flung herself on a cluster of grey
rocks at the edge of the river. After a few minutes, observed
closely, she climbed on the topmost rock. Dark greengage
moss trailed over it, an etching of olive fur. Small blue-
purple flowers clung to it, their primly purpled petals a
tiny textured mauve cover. Blue-purple, the colour of
heather, climbing close to the rock, holding on tight, blue-
brightening the leaden rock face.

Cressida ran her fingers over the rough plant-marked

stone. Long fingers, slightly roughened like the rock, working fingers with dark lines grazing the knuckles. She didn't use hand cream.

"It's not grey at all," Cressida said. "If you look underneath, it is pink and green."

She moved lightly, over and round the rock, stepping carefully, sure-footed, her dejected green jacket suddenly lit up, a light dazzle, flecking the stone surface.

"Come here, Kay," she called. "Touch them. Touch the flowers."

I walked over to the rock. We stood side by side. Were we breathing? Cressida looked intently at the mottled patterns. "You are right," I said. "It is pink and green."

Cressida drew her fingers over the lichen. A young girl tracing alphabet letters. She was not yet making words. I heard them, the words she was saying and the words she was not saying. In the distance the light lapping of water.

Soon it would be Christmas. Scarlet berries, purple chrysanthemums. Cressida and Charles would spend it together. Would the blue-purple flowers still climb close to the rock? I shivered. Would I remember the pink and the green?

Cressida traced the flower patterns on the crusty surface. Time and exposure had hardened the boulder on which small tufts of grass sprang up subversively infringing the cold taupe order. She pressed her hand over the green blades. We were taking our time.

I leant against the rock. The hard edge bit into me. I felt strong like the hard edge. The girl had brought me home. I felt I could ask her again. "I know what I want," I repeated. "I would like you to spend more time with me. Leaving you was a mistake."

"Let's go!" Cressida said curtly. "Charles will be back."

A week later Charles wrote a brief courteous note saying that he had talked to our daughter and she preferred to leave the situation as it was. After that I did not see Cressida or Charles for two years.

Today as I recalled the sun dappling the rock a sudden snowdrift flannelled Cressida's face. Her words drifted like whispers.

"Let's go. If you insist on climbing, Kay, I can't stop you. There's nothing to go back for is there? So we might as well climb."

We began the ascent.

We climbed for an hour without speaking. Was she thinking about Charles? I knew that in her grief she needed to climb alone but the weather had become treacherous. I was anxious for her safety. To be honest I was more concerned for my own. She was sure-footed, skilled, climbed regularly. I was out of practice, was wearing the wrong shoes. I looked down at my stupidly inadequate brogues. Why hadn't I packed climbing boots? All I had brought was a small hide overnight bag and a large empty suitcase. Could I persuade Cressida to fill it? Would she return south with me? If only for a few weeks.

She had not asked why the police had contacted me rather than her. She must resent that more than anything else.

It seemed that in Charles's wallet he still kept the engraved leather tags we gave each other years ago, when she was a baby, with a small photo, address and telephone number and the words: 'In emergency please contact'.

In the emergency they had leather-tagged me.

"Why a BUS?" Cressida's first words were half carried away on the wind.

"Absurd. I know. It seems absurd. Unfitting."

"Nothing fits," she said.

The climb grew steeper. She increased the distance between us. She began to run up the cliff. Rubble was raised from beneath her flying feet. The fine mist was turning to smouldering grey fog.

"Careful!" I yelled. "You are raising dust. I cannot see."

"Careful? I don't want to be careful."

More rubble, a small scattering of stones. I swerved to avoid them. I was perilously near the edge. My shoes on the snowy path would not grip, would not hold. My ankle twisted. I flailed, trying to grasp at boulders, bushes, anything. I began to fall. Someone was screaming.

Later Cressida said she thought she had screamed, not me.

I cannot recall pain equal to this pain. Sharp, spiked and shooting. A massive boulder had dropped on my twisted ankle, had smashed it I suppose but had pinioned it so that the rest of my body, splayed over the cliff edge, was held back by a boulderful of brittle bleeding bones and flesh.

It is possible that I fainted. Charles would have calmly said I had taken time out. When I opened my eyes Cressida was at my side. I had never before seen her appear shaken. Crises had always escalated her calmness. The news of Charles's death had frozen her features but my idiotic accident or whatever action she was contemplating was making her hands tremble.

"I thought I had lost you as well," she said. "I'll do a makeshift bandage. Here, hang on tight. I am drawing you back from the edge. I'll tear up my shirt. Now I'm going to run and get help."

She turned, then looked back at me.

"Kay, don't try and move will you?"

"It's OK," I said. 'I can't run away."

RADIO DRAMA

The Passenger in Pink

BY SALLY CLINE

CHARACTERS	
PASSENGER IN PINK	A woman. Early 40s. Sad. Reaching out.
WOMAN COMMUTER	A woman. Early 40s. Introspective. Emotionally withdrawn.
FATHER	A man. Late 30s.
JONNY	His son. Late teens. Bumptious.
TICKET MAN	Early 30s. Friendly.
THE PLAY IS SET IN:	Liverpool Street station A railway carriage Whittlesford station, Cambridgeshire

FADE UP. RAILWAY MUSIC.
"PASSENGER IN PINK" THEME TUNE.
HOLD.

CROSS-FADE TO EXTERIOR:
LIVERPOOL STREET STATION,
LONDON, IN THE RUSH HOUR. WE
HEAR TRAINS RUSH THROUGH.
MURMUR OF VOICES AS PASSENGERS
HASTILY CONSULT THE DEPARTURE
INDICATOR. SOUNDS OF TRAIN
TIMES AND PLATFORM NUMBERS
BEING CALLED OUT THROUGH THE
LOUDSPEAKER. GUARD'S WHISTLE.
SOUNDS OF RUSHING FOOTSTEPS.
FAR AWAY MAN'S VOICE CALLING

FATHER: OK son, that's the 5.05 over there, on platform
          9B. Remember it's a small platform at
          Whittlesford, so try and nab us a couple of seats
          in the first four carriages.

          SOUNDS OF BOY'S FOOTSTEPS
          DOWN PLATFORM. SOUNDS
          OF CARRIAGE DOORS OPENING AND
          SHUTTING. SOUNDS OF FATHER'S
          FOOTSTEPS FOLLOWING

JONNY: **(Calling)** Come down here, Dad! There's some
          left in this one.

          FADE. SOUNDS OF FATHER'S FEET
          CATCHING UP. DOOR OPENING
          AGAIN, SLAMMING SHUT. FADE UP.
          INTERIOR RAILWAY CARRIAGE

JONNY: Look, Dad, there's one opposite that lady in
          the awful pink dress... **(Breaks off as father**
          interrupts him)

FATHER: **(Interrupting fast. Reprovingly)**
          JONNY! *I can* see where the spare seats are.

(To the passenger in pink) Excuse me Madam is this your newspaper on the seat opposite?

PINK
PASSENGER:

(Dull dead monotone. Very slight working class accent) Paper? Yes, it's my paper. It definitely is my paper. Bought it when I set off this morning.

(Her voice fades slightly, becomes uncertain) I bought it after He'd gone. I didn't know what else to do... I thought a paper might...

(Her voice grows tearful, fades away)

FATHER:

(Interrupting briskly) Yes, I see. It *is* your paper. But please could you remove it so that one of us could sit down?

PASSENGER IN PINK PICKS UP PAPER, PUTS IT BACK ON SEAT. RUSTLE OF PAPER

PINK
PASSENGER:

No, I can't... you see I bought this paper, after He'd gone. I wondered if I should advertise for him, I wondered if thinking about an advert might take my mind off it. **(Pause. Sadly)**

It's hard to take my mind off it. I haven't been able to take my mind off it all day. I thought an advert in a paper might be an answer. I've never been good at answers. Mind you, I've never been good at questions. **(Pause)**

He didn't like you to ask questions, so that didn't matter much. **(Pause as she remembers the question)** Paper? Oh yes... I thought the paper might... well...

(Her voice trails away miserably. Then she makes an effort)

So I'm saving the seat with the paper.

SHE SIGHS WITH THE HUGE EFFORT OF HAVING COMMUNICATED THAT PIECE OF INFORMATION

FATHER: | **(Irritable and slightly discomforted at the Pink Passenger's randomness)**

Oh, I see. Well, we shall have to find other seats. Come on son, I can spot some by the window. Jonny don't wander off, more people are coming in now.

SOUNDS OF BOY WANDERING OFF. SOUNDS OF CARRIAGE DOOR OPENING. SOUNDS OF MORE PEOPLE ENTERING CARRIAGE. DOOR SLAMS. SOUNDS OF SCRABBLING FEET. MUTTERED APOLOGIES. NEWSPAPERS RUSTLE. VOICE OF WOMAN COMMUTER IS HEARD

WOMAN COMMUTER: | **(Middle aged, middle class voice. Slow, reflective, sometimes talks aloud, sometimes to herself)**

(Aloud to Father) Is this seat free?

FATHER: | No, I'm sorry. It's my son's. He seems to have wandered off for a minute.

JONNY: | **(Returning)** I was looking for a drinks trolley. Wish I had a coke or a cuppa something Dad! That woman with the awful pink... **(breaks off as Father nudges him)**...oh sorry... well she's gotta cuppa something.

(Pause) Look at her jiggling it in her hands. All nervy.

WOMAN COMMUTER: | **(To herself. Following boy's gaze to Passenger in Pink)** The boy is right. That woman in the gaudy pink dress looks nervy alright. She keeps touching that faded purple flower in her buttonhole... is it a tulip? Clenching and unclenching that paper cup. Giving herself away. Those string bags and plastic carriers will not contain her. **(Pause)**

Yes, giving herself away. Cheap at the price.
I am someone who has always avoided bargains.
Best to hurry by. Self-preservation, that's what
is needed.

PINK
PASSENGER:

I've saved *you* the seat. That one. Opposite.
Horrid having to stand all the way, isn't it?

WOMAN
COMMUTER:

(Aloud. Surprised) For me? The seat?
(Slight pause) Oh! Thank you.

(To herself) All that pink. Like an overgrown
blush. And the tangled red hair. It must be
henna. All that reaching out. Impossible to
ignore. **(Pause)**

The woman is what the grey days of winter
hinted as a summer possibility. But I am
someone who enjoys the snow. Nip in the air.
Tingle of frost. I should have hurried on before
the dead blue eyes fastened on me. They are
more green than blue. Blue jade? Dismal blue
jade? **(Pause)**

Faces on a train are easily forgotten… why
cannot I take my eyes from yours?

Your cheeks are grey, smudged like the smoke
smudged window.

PINK
PASSENGER:

It's all grey outside the window. Funny when
it's only just gone five. It'll be dark when we
get there. **(Her voice droops)** I don't want to
think about that.

WOMAN
COMMUTER:

(Aloud. Briskly) Grey, yes. The evenings are
turning in.

(To herself. Pensively) Grey, yes like your
cheeks. You know I am watching you. It will
not do. It cannot happen. I have to preserve my
ignorance of you. I have to deny my knowledge
of you. I cannot have that. I do not want that.

(Pause. Then abruptly repeats herself)

No, I do not want that.

PINK
PASSENGER:

(Hopeless voice) Want some coffee? There's a drop of coffee left. I expect it's cold though. Paper cups are hopeless.

WOMAN
COMMUTER:

(Aloud. Trying to appear disinterested) No thanks. No coffee. **(Pause)**

(To herself) I'd buy you another one. A hot one. But it would not end there. You would plan picnics. Read me out the headlines. Tell me what your mother said.

SOUNDS OF QUIET SOB FROM PINK PASSENGER

Oh no! You're not going to cry. **(Panic in voice)** Surely I have got a book in my briefcase. I had a thriller on the downward journey this morning.

SOUNDS OF BRIEFCASE OPENING, SNAPPING SHUT. WOMAN COMMUTER TAKES OUT BOOK. SOUNDS OF PAGES TURNING.

PINK
PASSENGER:

(Suddenly alert. Sharply) I haven't read that one. Good ending is it?

WOMAN
COMMUTER:

(Aloud. Nervously) I don't know. I haven't finished it.

(To herself) You are lying. You finished it on the journey down. You finished it three stops before Liverpool Street this morning.

PINK
PASSENGER:

(Dully) I had a Mystery this morning. I finished it on the journey down. Finished it three stops before Liverpool Street. Couldn't keep my mind on it. Too upset. **(Pause)** *He* used to bring me Mysteries from the library. Ever so often. He won't be doing that any more. **(Long pause. Stifling tears. Pulls herself together. Tries to be friendly)** Your book good then?

WOMAN COMMUTER:	**(To herself. Backing away psychologically)** Don't ask to borrow my book. It won't help you read my mind. Or make up yours. There is a table between us carefully delineating our rights.
PINK PASSENGER:	It wasn't right coming back… but I couldn't stay… there was nothing to come back for… but there was nothing to stay for. **(Low tremulous voice)** I had to catch the 5.05.

NO ANSWER. SOUNDS OF PAGES TURNING. MUTTERS OF OTHER PASSENGERS. PEOPLE COUGH. JONNY WHINES. FATHER ADMONISHES HIM QUIETLY. THEN AN UNCOMFORTABLE SILENCE

PINK PASSENGER:	**(Louder)** I *had* to catch the 5.05.

STILL NO ANSWER

(Louder still) You see I had to… I mean you can't keep staying in London, not on the platform, not when it isn't your home.

SOUNDS OF PINK PASSENGER CHOKING BACK TEARS

I don't know where my home is now. Not without Him to get back to. He used to say "The 5.05 is a good train. A useful train. Much the best one to get back." And now…

(Her voice trails off despairingly)

WOMAN COMMUTER:	**(Aloud. Embarrassed. Brisk)** The 5.05 is a good train. A useful train. Much the best one to get back.

(To herself. Panic rising) She has marked me out. She knows I always catch the 5.05 on Fridays. She has obviously been following my movements for weeks.

PINK PASSENGER: (**Aloud. Sadly**) He'd been like a cat for weeks, following my movements round the house, his eyes watching to see if I'd jump this way or that. Right up to John's Death he was like that. (He'd never taken to our Lil's John. But The Death made Him jumpy. Made us all jumpy). After The Death, he stopped watching me like a cat, took a turn for the quiet, then this morning he moved out. It was very sudden. So was John's Death. I couldn't think what to do. I took a train to London. Thought it best. Couldn't think of anything else to do.

WOMAN COMMUTER: (**Aloud. Hopeless tone. Uncertain what to say**) Always the best.

(**Abruptly. Brighter tone**) London is an exciting city to work in... (**Her voice trails away**)

(**To herself**) Is it? Why do I no longer find it exciting? I haven't wanted to work there since the day he left.

(**Pause**)

(**To herself**) Why doesn't that boy's Father say something? That Jonny's Dad must be listening. How could he help it? He must understand. He must have neighbours like the woman in the silk dress. Their neighbours must use henna. Can't he see that I need help?

PINK PASSENGER: (**Tonelessly**) Can't they see that I need help? The neighbours I mean. I went to the neighbours first. But they wouldn't listen. They didn't understand. They couldn't see that I needed help. What could I do except go to London?

WOMAN COMMUTER: (**Aloud. Trying to be cheerful. Not really wanting to engage**) Good thing, going to London. Can be a great help.

PINK PASSENGER:	**(As if she has not heard)** I really wanted someone to hold my hand. **(Long pause) ABSOLUTE SILENCE IN CARRIAGE** You do after someone goes… it is like a Death… know what I mean? **SILENCE. FADE. SOUNDS OF MUSIC, SAME "PASSENGER IN PINK" THEME MUSIC. FADE UP INTERIOR SAME RAILWAY CARRIAGE. SOUNDS OF SWEETS RUSTLING**
PINK PASSENGER:	Want a toffee? Here I'll give you one. **MORE SOUNDS OF PAPER BAG OF SWEETS RUSTLING. PASSENGER IN PINK HOLDS OUT HER HAND, SOUNDS OF WOMAN COMMUTER'S SHARP INTAKE OF BREATH.** I got them in London. Here you are. **(Stretches out hand)**
WOMAN COMMUTER:	**(To herself. Violently)** Take back your hand. I cannot touch you. I cannot touch anyone. I know the rules on trains. I have a Network card. South East region. Valid until next March. I have read the small print. Know the card is issued subject to the appropriate conditions. Know you have to keep within the Board's Conditions of Carriage for Passengers and Luggage. Know a passenger has to keep within the Excess Rules and Restrictions. Touching another passenger's hands, even one sitting opposite sharing the same table, would be excessive, exceeding the limits. You do not spend money on a Network card and flaunt the regulations. **(Pause. Deep breath)** You must take your hand away.

	(Aloud) No thank you. No toffee.
JONNY:	**(Interrupting loudly)** You can have my hand miss if I can have one of your toffees.
FATHER:	**(Shocked and cross)** Jonny! Let go of the lady's hand. Settle down. Let me borrow your Walkman and you get your book out.
	SOUNDS OF "PASSENGER IN PINK" THEME ON THE BOY'S PERSONAL STEREO. SOUNDS OF PAGES TURNING. BOOK SNAPS OPEN AND CLOSED. FADE. FADE UP. MORE SOUNDS OF PAGES TURNING AND RAILWAY NOISES.
WOMAN COMMUTER:	**(Aloud. Practical tone)** I must finish my thriller before we reach Whittlesford. Have to leave time to gather my belongings together.
PINK PASSENGER:	**(Sad monotone)** I didn't pack a bag. I couldn't seem to gather my belongings together. You know how it is?
WOMAN COMMUTER:	**(Unwillingly. Quiet voice)** I know how it is.
	(Desperate shot in the dark) I expect you've got relations in London? You don't need to take so much then.
PINK PASSENGER:	**(More alert, bright voice)** I have. Lil the eldest. And Mum. And of course there was Lil's John. Until The Death.
	(Firmer voice. Tinged with resentment) Lil always hated Him. John didn't like Him either. Though he didn't say so, not in as many words. Lil would have been pleased He'd upped and left. Good riddance she'd have said. Not your sort! Not your sort at all. That's what she used to say. He *was* my sort... well I thought so at the beginning. I thought I was *his* sort. Not that I know what his sort was. It's obvious now.

(She gives a pained laugh. Grows sad again)
I'd always wanted us to be happy. Being a
couple is supposed to make you happy. It wasn't
just what Mum said. All those book writers,
"Woman's Weekly" and "She" and "Best", they
all tell you how to go about it, how to be happy.
They say you can have rows and still be happy.
Still be a happy couple. A proper couple. With
indoor plants and using the timer on your video
to get the best out of life.

(Pause) Of course we had rows. Well, you do
don't you? You can't go all those years and not
have troubles. **(Pause. Reflective voice)** We
had troubles. Mainly we'd fight about the babies.

WOMAN   **(Aloud, with obvious relief)** Oh! You have
COMMUTER: got babies! Too many I expect. Babies can be a
                 lot of trouble.

(To herself. Angrily) How can I talk like that? I
know nothing about babies. I've never had a baby.

(Pauses. To herself. Reflectively) Was that
part of the trouble?

PINK   **(Angrily. Aloud)** How can you talk like that?
PASSENGER: You can't know nothing about babies. They
                 aren't no trouble, not if they was your own.
                 (Pauses. Sadder voice) Part of the trouble
                 was I couldn't have a baby. Not one of my
                 own. He minded that. Thought I'd done him
                 out of something. So we rowed, see?

WOMAN   **(Aloud)** I see.
COMMUTER:

(To herself) I see.

Yes I see it now. We rowed. "You wouldn't be so
damn selfish if you'd had babies!" That's what he
said. Unintelligent! Infantile! Sexist! Insensitive!
That's what he was.

(Pause. Half laughing. Softer tone)
Intelligent... adult... rarely sexist... sensitive...
that's what he was. (Pause) But he didn't
understand. Rows? Of course there were
rows. Rows and reconciliations. Rows and
recriminations. Rows and regret. How the rows
rankle still. How one never forgets. (Pause.
Sadly) But he never understood how I felt.

PINK
PASSENGER:

He never understood how I felt. For years I'd
gaze at babies in supermarkets, their Mums
pushing those trollies, those special ones for
babies, pretending I didn't mind, pretending one
of them was mine. You know how it is...

WOMAN
COMMUTER:

(Aloud. Musing) I know how it is.

(To herself) For years I'd gaze at babies
in supermarkets pretending I didn't mind.
Pretending that one of them was mine.

(Very harshly) What a pretence! As soon as I
bumped into one, I hastily took a can of beans
from the shelf, protected myself from a passing
baby with a can of beans, rich in fibre, rich in
protein, a valuable part of a nutritious diet, a
well-balanced life. Yes, that's what a can of beans
can do. It can make you feel good, help you to
become well-balanced, not like a can of babies,
not even like one baby. What a pretence! One
baby would have been one too many.

(Pause. Then less angry but cold) Baked
beans are free from artificial colours and
preservatives, leave you free, set you free.
Babies tie you up, tie you down, leave you
preserved, withered and dried up. Babies touch
you, and need you, they spill stuff over you, grab
on to bits of you. Babies are sticky and wet.
They slobber, they're sickly, they slurp and they
shriek, they soften you up, they slice you open.
You are never the same after being with babies.

I cannot have babies. I cannot touch anyone.
I am pristine and perfect, pedantic and polished.
Like sharp glass I cut. Babies are not safe with
me. I keep my clothes clean, I iron out the
creases. I am someone who abhors loud voices
and vomit. I cannot be held on to, I cannot be
held back. Babies need cradling. You do it by
contact. I'd do it better by digging their graves.
At least when you're digging, you are allowed to
wear wellingtons.

(Aloud. Trying to sound rational) You are
never the same after being with babies. It gets
worse and worse.

PINK
PASSENGER: It gets worse and worse, the not having babies. It
got worse and worse, over the baby, not having
one I mean. The rows went on for nearly a year.

WOMAN
COMMUTER: **(To herself)** The rows went on for nearly a year.
Nothing new, nothing different. "You are selfish!
You are cold! Babies would change you. You
are selfish! You are cold! Babies make a family."
That's what he said... All repetition and no release.
All physicality and no freedom. He wanted me
to walk in a jungle of Fuzzy Felt. He wanted me
to buy alphabet biscuits. He wanted my babies
more than he wanted my mind or myself. Babies
become children. Family problems, ancient habits
and that's if you're lucky. Tedious troubles that tie
you together. You begin to rely on family tortures
to stop yourself falling apart. Are families a source
of dietary fibre? Are families tasty? Wholesome?
Nutritious? Or are families blanks? Well-
designed blank interiors? Led by mothers, sunk
into their veins, knotted blue with despair, errors,
misjudgements. Being with babies is like having
a plastic bag placed over your head. Tied up with
string, knotted under your chin. Knotted blue
with despair, errors, misjudgements. You begin to
suffocate, start to shriek, you loosen the knot.

Someone tells you that you are comfortable. You are doing a good job. You are being a mother. You are touching your children.

(Sarcastically) How touching that is! Being a mother. They push your head back inside the bag. Not brutally but firmly. Firmly and tenderly. Glad that you are comfortable. Glad that you are doing a good job in hard times. Being a mother. Touching your children. Suffocating them with love.

(Pause)

Suffocating yourself! But not so badly that anyone would notice. Stifling the rows, so that no-one would notice.

PINK
PASSENGER: **(Aloud. Wearily)** I kept stifling the rows, so that no-one would notice. But they went on for almost a year. Well I think it was about eight, no, nine months. Then suddenly, almost like it was one day, He just stopped fighting with me. **(Pause)** He went out on a trip one night... he's a long-distance lorry driver, always away on trips... when he came back he had this baby slung over his shoulder. **(Slight pause)** He never did say where he got it. Just handed it over with some money to get baby things and extra food. It was really little. In nappies, it was, tiny spiky hair and tiny fingers. I kept counting them to make sure it was real, and wondering where he got it. He threatened to half kill me if I asked any questions. First I was worried that the police would come. But they never did. Nobody come. Then I worried about what the neighbours would say. *He* didn't worry. "Tell them it's your Mother's baby! Tell them it's your sister's baby... or your brother's baby. Tell them anything! Tell them you're minding it. You are, aren't you? Minding it. You'd better bloody mind it." That's what He said. Angry, he was. Angry that I'd said anything at all.

He didn't like you to speak up. I tried to reason with him. I told him I didn't have a brother, I told him my sisters all had babies; I told him Mum was too old to have any more babies, but he wouldn't listen.

WOMAN
COMMUTER:

(Aloud. Quietly) He wouldn't listen.

(To herself. Angrily) He wouldn't listen. I told him my sisters all had babies. We could spend our time with them. I told him I was too old to be a mum. I told him I was too old to have babies. I told him you are never the same after being with babies. **(Pause)** That wasn't the reason and he saw through the lie. He said I was cold. He said I was frigid. He said I did not know how to touch where it mattered. He said I lived somewhere else and went through the motions. **(Pause)** Motions? Emotions? I don't have them, I don't want them. I cannot... I will not... I never could... answer up... measure up... stand up... certainly not to be counted... Mothers do all of those things, then those things count for nothing. **(Pause)** Mothers live in locked rooms without doors. A mother lives in a room with no door, with only one window, that looks out into another locked room, with no door and only one window. **(Urgently. Emphatically)** I have to look out. I have to get out. I have to reach the fresh air. What I cannot do is I cannot reach out. I am heavily into veils and withdrawal. I should forget the names of my children, carefully overlook each of their birthdays, fail to get in touch when they moved away from home. I cannot keep in touch because... **(Slight pause)** because I cannot keep in touch. If you look at me closely, it is obvious at first, but after a while nobody notices...

PINK
PASSENGER:

After a while nobody notices, the neighbours I mean, whether you have a new baby or not.

People are always bringing things in and out down our way. One more baby isn't such a surprise. I needn't have worried.

WOMAN COMMUTER: **(Aloud. Trying to pay some attention)** You needn't have worried. The worries come after you have babies. You have to be what they call a good mother.

PINK PASSENGER: I tried to be a good mother. But it's hard work when it's not your own. When you don't know where it's been. It made him happy so I thought we'd be happy. But we weren't. He didn't pay me any attention. Sort of fastened on the baby. Sometimes he'd sling her over his shoulder, pack her a little bag, and if he wasn't driving the lorry that day, he'd turn to me and say:

"We're off for the day. See you tonight." I never knew where he went, or what he did with her. I didn't like to ask. He didn't like you asking questions. Put him in a mood. But he went off with that baby slung over his shoulders, singing like he used to when he first courted me, all those years ago. Then they'd come back in time for their tea, and he'd stop singing just as soon as he was inside the door. He never liked me to leave the house when he was out with that baby. "Don't you go anywhere!" he'd say. "Know what I mean? Don't you go visiting anyone while her and me is out. Your place is at home. See that you stay there. Don't you go out." He'd repeat it several times. Then he'd say "We'll be back for our tea." **(Slight pause)** So I never did go out. Although I wanted to. Seeing as how I had a day off. I could have caught the train. I could have gone to Lil's or Mum's. I could have gone to one of the others. The youngest, she used to ask me over a lot. **(Pause)** But I knew it was best not to cross him. **(Pause)** He called her Rose. The baby. That was the name he gave her.

He'd say with a laugh "You've got a Lily in your
family and now I've got myself a Rose." But I
hadn't. I hadn't got a lily. She wasn't my lily!
Anyway, none of us called her that; too fancy by
half, she was always plain Lil. The truth was, I
didn't like Lil much. I didn't even feel she was
family, even though she was. The truth was, I
didn't like that Rose much either. She was a sort
of spiteful baby, reminded me of… oh, I don't
know…I got those funny feelings about her… but
He never noticed. He thought she was all roses.

WOMAN
COMMUTER:

(Only half listening) All roses was it? Roses all
the way?

PINK
PASSENGER:

(Very alert) Roses? More like trouble. Trouble
seems to bloom in families doesn't it? First that
strange death; our Lil's John being buried with a
Verdict, after his Funny Do; then *Him* running
off, taking the baby, slinging that Rose over his
shoulder, going for good. Mum would say there's
got to be a third. Always comes in threes, Mum
says. **(Pause)** Well I'm a Disaster! I haven't got
a life now but I don't expect that counts. Not
like Him running off. That counts alright. Not
like Lil's John dying after his Funny Do. That
certainly counted.

WOMAN
COMMUTER:

(Drawn in. Fascinated in spite of herself)
Funny Do?

PINK
PASSENGER:

Well, it was funny, sort of weird the way John
died. One minute he was leaving the house, all
smooth and cool… (he used to sell computer
stationery, all floppies and formatting, and
he always acted like a salesman, all oily and
smart)… so there he was getting in his bright red
Fiesta, starting it up, nipping up their drive…
(they don't live in a terrace like the rest of us.
John's always had money, made it in computer
stationery. Mum says that's why Lil married him,
"computer cop-out" that's what Mum says.)

So there he was nipping up their drive when suddenly… wham! bang! smash! … this great horrible lorry comes charging straight into his red Fiesta. Well that's what Lil said. She was the only witness, not that she could talk much at the time. She was all weeping and screaming and said she didn't really see what happened, she didn't get the lorry's number plate, just heard these crashes. Seems the lorry driver smashed him up head on. Seems he smashed the whole of the front of the car. **(Pause)**

It went up in flames. Lil got hysterical and by the time the police got there, the lorry had gone, never stopped nor nothing, and John was dead.

WOMAN
COMMUTER:

(Still interested) How did Lil take it?

PINK
PASSENGER:

Funny thing about Lil. Right up to the Inquest, she was in ever such a state. Mum had to stay with her half the night. Then once the Inquest was over and they'd brought in this verdict of accidental death, or was it death-by-person-or-persons unknown, I can't quite remember, still once there was a verdict, Lil took a turn for the better. My youngest sister, she says it's the money Lil got. From John's insurance policy. Computer salesmen, they're always insured. They believe anything can happen! That's what John used to say. "Anything can happen," that's what he said. Said it a lot. **(Pause)** Well, for once John was right! **(Pause. Wistfully)** Ever such a lot of money it was. More than any of us have ever dreamt of. **(Pause)** I don't know whether Mum was right about Lil, about it being the money that cheered her up. Lil's always been an odd one… Ever so close. You never *did* know what was going on…She says she's going away now, a long way away, to make a fresh start. Mum can't understand it. Our family never goes away. I've gone the furthest and that's only to Whittlesford.

(**Pause**) It will be funny her going away. What
with Him gone away this morning, gone with that
baby, that Rose, slung over his shoulder. What with
your sister going, and Him gone, and that baby
gone, there's not much of a family left to rely on.

WOMAN
COMMUTER:

I suppose Lil could rely on your family to all go
to John's funeral? Hard things funerals...

PINK
PASSENGER:

(**Very intent and serious**) The hard thing was
I had to go on my own. *He* wouldn't come.
Didn't like Lil. (**Pause**) Well, said he didn't.
Didn't like John either. No doubt about that!
Laughed like a drain when I told him the news.
I thought that was going a bit too far. He said
he was tired. Wouldn't go to the funeral. He'd
been on two long-distance shifts. Had his lorry
in a breakdown... said he was far too tired to
go with me to London. Said he'd stay with
the baby. I said "No, I'll take that Rose to the
funeral." Sort of cheers you up to take a baby to
a funeral. He wouldn't have none of it. Angry,
he got real angry. "You leave that Rose here!" he
shouted. "Leave her here, or I'll kill yer!" He was
always a bit hasty. (**Pause**) When I got back from
the funeral, he was very quiet, kept laughing to
himself but he wouldn't talk to me. Started doing
everything for the baby himself. He wouldn't
let me touch her. Well, he gets these turns
sometimes, so I let it pass. I kept hoping we were
going to be a happy family. A couple and a baby,
happy like in the ads. (**Pause. Sadly**) I never
wanted anyone but him. Know what I mean?

WOMAN
COMMUTER:

(**Aloud**) I know what you mean. (**To herself**)
I know what you mean. I never wanted anyone
but him. But I never wanted what he wanted.
He wanted us to be a "happy family".

PINK
PASSENGER:

I thought *he* wanted us to be a happy family. *I*
never wanted anything but for us to be a happy
family. So I just let it pass. (**Pause**)

	Then last night he told me to pack a bag for the baby and not to ask any questions. I knew something was up! You can tell when you've lived a long time with someone… **(Her voice trails away)**
WOMAN COMMUTER:	**(Aloud but as if to herself)** You can tell when you've lived a long time with someone. You know something's up. You even know what is up. But it is probably something you don't want to face. We had lived together so long that I never dreamed… I never guessed…
PINK PASSENGER:	I never dreamed… I never guessed… I never thought… not that he'd go. **(Pause)**
	Then this morning, he just told me, straight out, after he'd moaned about the porridge… (he always said it was lumpy)… told me that he was going, taking that Rose and going and that I needn't expect him back. "Never," he said. He said it aloud. "Never," he said. **(Her voice is in shock)** He is not a man who changes his mind. Never has been. So I had to believe him. **(Pause)**
WOMAN COMMUTER:	**(To herself)** You had to believe him. **(Pause. Obviously shaken)** You have to believe them if they won't change their minds. You have to be hard. You have to be resolute. You mustn't look in their eyes.
PINK PASSENGER:	His eyes were all glittery, like he could see something I couldn't see. On the horizon. Something in his future. **(Pause. Very sadly)** I haven't got a future. I couldn't see anything after he went. I just went on crying. I've been crying on and off all day. I rang the youngest but she wasn't in, so I thought I'd go and see Lil. Well, that's what your family is for even if you don't get on. Then I thought of her having had that Death, and of John's Funny Do, and her good fortune with all that money, and her about to go off, and I thought it's no good my going down and crying.

It will only upset her. **(Pause. Big sigh)** You can't rely on them. Families. Can you? It never works out. So I didn't go and see Lil, and I didn't go and see Mum. She'd have been as mad as hell, and ever so upset. It wouldn't have helped me, not seeing Mum today. Not a lot of point. I just went to Liverpool Street and stayed as long as you can on the platform… **(Voice trails away)**

WOMAN COMMUTER: **(Aloud. Unwillingly drawn in. Softly, paying attention)** Of course I know. Yes, I know.

PINK PASSENGER: **(Dead tone)** But they make you go home.

WOMAN COMMUTER: **(Still attentive)** Of course, I know. **(To herself. Angrily)** Isn't anyone else listening? Isn't it anyone else's responsibility? What right has that man, the one with the boy, to put a Sony Walkman in his ears? What right has he got to turn her sound down? To turn her voice out?

SOUNDS OF MUSIC. "PASSENGER IN PINK" THEME. SOUNDS OF TAPPING TO MUSIC

PINK PASSENGER: Yes, they make you go home.

WOMAN COMMUTER: **(Aloud. Trying to be cheerful)** Best to go home. It's always best to go home

(To herself) What a traitor you are. How can you lie to her? **(Pause)** But how can you tell her the truth in a railway carriage? How can you tell the truth to yourself?

(Pause. Angrily) Do you want to hear that truth? **(Pause. Then more moderately)** Whatever you tell, whatever you say, it will only be your truth…

PINK PASSENGER: **(Softly)** They don't tell you the truth. They don't tell you it's hard to go home.

They don't care if you can't go home... if you
are afraid. They don't listen if you tell them.
They stuff up their ears. They switch on their
tellies. They listen to the Top Ten. They don't
care if you are right down there at the bottom.

**SOUNDS OF MUSIC. SOUNDS OF
TAPPING TO MUSIC**

They don't want to know why you can't go
home when you've had a terrible jolt, when your
life has changed.

WOMAN
COMMUTER:

(Aloud. Harshly. Again distancing herself)
All those terrible jolts. All those changes at
stations. Makes it hard to read on trains doesn't it?

(To herself. Softly) I should put down my
book. Go on. Talk to me. I am listening. I do
care. But I can't show it. I don't know how to.

PINK
PASSENGER:

(Desperate voice) I don't know how to walk
up the path to the front door.

WOMAN
COMMUTER:

(To herself. Desperate voice) Would you
like me to walk home with you? Walk up the
front path. Take your key, open the front door,
go in. Read the paper while you put the kettle
on. Tell you about my day. Ask you about
yours. I want to say: "Would you like to borrow
my company?" like I would say: "Would you
like to borrow my book or my umbrella?" But
I can't say it. (I can't say "Would you like to
borrow my baby?" either, because there are no
babies in stock.) I cannot say any of it because
I know it will not stop there. I told you earlier;
don't ask to borrow my book. It will not help
you read my mind. Or make up yours. In
any case, I am not a lending library. I fear the
rain. I have a life of my own. **(Long pause)**
I did want to say it, so that not being a lending
library is not the whole reason.

PINK
PASSENGER:

(Sadly) They never give you any reason, not the whole reason, for not listening, when you're in trouble. You go on telling them, and they go on not listening. **(Pause)** I thought of advertising for Him or for that baby. In the local paper. Perhaps in the classified. They've got a cheap rate. But then I thought, I haven't really got the money, and it wouldn't do any good. **(Long pause)** You can't advertise for anyone to walk up the path to the front door with you.

WOMAN
COMMUTER:

(To herself. Bitter and realistic) I do not know how to walk up the path to the front door with you. I have never done that for anyone. I cannot hold your hand. I am holding on to my book.

PAGES RUSTLE

I understand books. It is people that fluster me. People and babies. **(Pause)**

It's never the same after being with babies. It's never the same after being without.

PINK
PASSENGER:

It's never the same after being with babies. Not when you've been without. So I thought after he'd found us that baby, it would feel different. I thought we'd be blissful, just like it says in the maggies. I never thought he'd leave me. You don't do you? Not after all those years. Not after finding us a baby. **(Pause)** It comes without any warning. You don't get an amber light like crossing the road. Leaves you sort of flat doesn't it? You never get used to it.

WOMAN
COMMUTER:

(Aloud. Determined to break away from the woman's spell) Look out of the window. It's sort of flat isn't it? You never get used to it. All those fields flat. Flat and rather bleak. Look out of the window; field after field, station after station. All of it flat. The train pulling in, the train pulling out. What would happen to them if they jumped too soon, is a forgone conclusion.

See that girl with the purple punky hair...
the same colour as that mauve tulip you are
wearing... she left it late. Had to spring out
while the train was moving. *She* took a risk. I
never jump out when the train is moving. I am
too old to change. Stops. Or my life. It would
be rash to try and make changes.

**SOUNDS OF TRAIN COMING TO HALT.
FADE. FADE UP INTERIOR SAME
RAILWAY CARRIAGE**

**SOUND OF ELECTRONIC
ANOUNCEMENT:**

Change here. Next stop Whittlesford. Move
into the first four carriages. It's a small platform.

WOMAN
COMMUTER:

(Briskly) Nearly there.

PINK
PASSENGER:

(Sadly) Nearly there. **(Pause)** I live right
at the top of Farmer's Lane. Ever such a haul.
Some days I bring the bike. I can't remember
about this morning. I can't remember whether
I brought the bike or not. I was too upset,
couldn't concentrate. Kept thinking about
Him. Worrying about that baby. **(Pause)** I
think I shall have to sport a cab. I suppose I
could. Sport a cab I mean, I've only got myself
to think of now.

(Starts to cry, tries to recover)

WOMAN
COMMUTER:

(Aloud. Firmly) Do that. Sport a cab. Much
the best.

**SOUNDS OF TRAIN SLOWING DOWN.
TRAIN GRINDS TO HALT**

(Aloud. Briskly) Here we are then.
Whittlesford. Goodbye.

**SOUNDS OF DOORS OPENING,
SLAMMING SHUT. PLATFORM
NOISES. FADE.**

FADE UP EXTERIOR WHITTLESFORD
PLATFORM. SOUNDS OF ONE PAIR
OF FOOTSTEPS DOWN PLATFORM.
WOMAN COMMUTER GREETS TICKET
ATTENDANT A BIT NERVOUSLY

WOMAN
COMMUTER:
**(Aloud. Nervously. Not her brisk cold
self)** Well, um… hello, Joe.

TICKET MAN:
(Warm, friendly voice) Hello, Miss. Your bike
is alright, Miss. Kept my beady eye on it. You
alright, Miss? Thought you looked very upset
this morning. Not like yourself at all.

WOMAN
COMMUTER:
(Distinctly rattled) Oh this morning… well I…

TICKET MAN:
(Cutting in) It was such a scrum I didn't say
anything at the time. But after you'd gone, I
thought, funny that, you looked like you'd had a
bit of a jolt.

WOMAN
COMMUTER:
(Aloud. Startled. Nervy) Oh! Funny that…
this morning? Oh yes, this morning. **(Long
pause. Sad voice)** I had forgotten about the
bike. I thought I should have to sport a cab.
Only got myself to… **(Breaks off sentence
rapidly. Tries to pull herself together.
More briskly)** Thanks. Cheers, Joe.

SOUNDS OF HER FEET WALKING TO
THE BIKE RAILS

(To herself) Where did I put the bike lock?
(Pause. Sighs aloud. Then to herself) I'd
better put it in third. It's a long haul to the top.
Then on to the path. **(To herself)** I don't know
how to walk up the path to the front door.

SOUNDS OF "PASSENGER IN PINK"
THEME

MUSIC TO END PLAY